Deceit by Design

Roz Potgieter

First published in 2020 by Roz Potgieter

www.rozpotgieter.com

Cilento Publishing, Sydney Australia

This novel is entirely a work of fiction. The names, characters and incidents portrayed in it are the product of the author's imagination. Any resemblance to actual persons, living or dead, events or localities is entirely coincidental.

ISBN 978-0-6487566-4-4 (Print)

ISBN 978-0-6487566-5-1 (eBook)

Cover design by Cristy Zinn

Internal design by Sarah Ayres

Roz Potgieter

DEDICATION

My precious Mom, Sheila Worraker (1931-2017).

Thank you for the thousands of hours on the phone going over every word (except the sex scenes and profanities!).

Your absolute belief in my ability, your unwavering love, support and guidance, and your enthusiasm throughout my writing journey gave me the strength to succeed.

I hope I've made you proud, Mom – it's officially been published! I've left an open copy on the coffee table in the white lounge for you to read.

I love and miss you more than words can say.

Chapter 1

The headline screamed at him from the grocery store window. Challenging him. Mocking him. The urge to smash his fist through the shopfront glass to the paper it protected swelled inside his chest, where the desire to shatter something had been getting stronger every day since the news had first swept through the small city of Champaign, Illinois, sending its mindless inhabitants into a delirium of patriotic fervour.

He made to take a step forward but was forced to stop almost immediately as an early-morning jogger breezed between the window and his face. The jogger halted in his stride and backtracked. A moment later, the man's reflection appeared in the window next to his, sporting a wide smile.

The jogger's chest rose and fell several times before he spoke. 'Yowsers – it'll be huge! Gonna bring this place to a standstill, huh?'

You're already standing still, you mindless, shit-licking dumbass.

The urge came howling back again. He strode forward once more, this time aiming for the shop's open door. Newspapers were stacked on the cashier's counter. Without a word, he picked up a copy of the *Champaign Chronicle*, paid, and left, the paper rolled up in his fist like a baton.

Once he was home, sitting at his desk, he finally read it. The headline took up half the front page, with an exclamation mark awarded to each of Champaign's favourite daughters. Even though he knew it would just be a rehash of everything he'd heard all week, he read the article from end to end.

Champaign Chronicle

May 29th, 2010

TRIUMPHANT TRIO TOUCH DOWN TOMORROW!!!

Kirsten Wells

Champaign's Golden Trio will touch down in style as they get together with former classmates for their tenth school reunion, in collaboration with the school's one hundredth anniversary. The Trio have certainly put Champaign on the map – how many schools can lay claim to an Olympic gold, an imminent Oscar, and a Grammy?

Astonishingly, all three girls are from the same class! 'The proceedings have been planned, right down to the finest details, and we'll all be there to welcome our new-found celebrities,' Principal Josh Templeton stated.

The article ended with the same old drivel about their respective successes: Leigh O'Rielly and her gold medal dominance in Beijing; Gabriella Cantrello and her Oscar nomination for her performance in *Oceanos Finale*; and, of course, the Grammy award-winner Anastasia Carlyle-Benson, affectionately known as Ana B, about to embark on her European tour after topping all charts in the UK, USA, Europe, South Africa, and Australasia.

He crumpled the *Chronicle* into a ball and hurled it towards his wastepaper basket, watching as it bounced off the rim. He sighed.

His gaze swivelled to the mirror on the wall. He liked what he saw. Everything, apart from his dark, wavy hair, was hard and angular – not an ounce of excess anywhere.

Chiselled? Was that the word the gym rats used? It was a good word. It made him feel dangerous.

Big, huh? Y'all ain't seen nothin' yet.

He flexed and smiled.

'Tick-tock, tick-tock. Watch the clock; oh, how it shall rock...'

Chapter 2

Flags and people lined the streets as the stretch limousine glided through the city centre, making Leigh O'Rielly shake her head in wonderment. She glanced across at her two companions, happy to see they were equally stunned by the carnival-like display.

Flying in from Melbourne, she'd been the last to arrive at Champaign's only airport. Gabriella, arriving from LA, had naturally been the first one home, but it irked Leigh more than she would care to admit that Ana, coming in on the red eye from London, had beaten her to second place. They'd last seen each other in person four years ago, on holiday in Hawaii, but had kept in constant virtual contact. That's why it'd been such a surprise to discover Ana had changed to an earlier flight without telling her.

Putting aside her annoyance, Leigh asked the question that had been bothering her since getting into the limo. 'I thought Marco would be meeting us at the airport?'

'Don't you worry about Marco,' Ana replied. 'He's waiting for us at the school.'

Leigh frowned. In her mind – and no doubt Ana's as well – the highlight of the whole event was the chance to catch up with their favourite teacher. Early on in their school days, he'd seen something special in all three of them. He had moulded them into the women they'd become, slipping into the role of friend, mentor, and confidante in the process.

Amidst the euphoria of an adoring crowd, the limousine made its way down Belmont Avenue, turned the corner into Oak Street and pulled into the parking lot of Brentwood Park High School. As the limo slowed, the red carpet came into view. It flowed through the grandeur of the school's entrance, towards the magnificent Victorian architecture beyond, winding past sprawling lawns and majestic oak trees. The applause was deafening as they stepped out of the limo.

'Would you have ever imagined this in your wildest dreams, Leigh?' Gabriella asked, clutching her fascinator firmly against the wind.

'Never!'

'Hey, the three musketeers were always destined for fame,' said Ana, with an infectious laugh.

Leigh took her companions by the hands. Together, they walked along the red carpet and ascended the stairs of the administration building, towards the beaming Marco Carrera. He enveloped them in a hug.

'My girls!' he exclaimed, through the cacophony of the crowd. Without further ado, he escorted them to the staffroom, where the principal and most of their former teachers were waiting. His excitement was palpable as he briefed them about the formalities of the day. They were to open the assembly as the school's honoured guests, then the principal would deliver his address, and the Valedictorian and Salutatorian would give a motivational message and prayer respectively. The afternoon would end in a cocktail party scheduled for 6 p.m. Marco assured them that there would be plenty of time to acclimatise to their celebrity status.

+ + +

Shelagh O'Rielly sat in the front row, never taking her eyes off her daughter once throughout the entire ceremony. When the speeches were over, Leigh bounced towards her and wrapped her in a warm embrace.

'I've missed you,' she said, her face buried in her mother's shoulder.

'I'm so proud of you,' Shelagh said. 'Seeing you on that stage… you've worked so hard, darling. I'm ecstatic the world finally gets to see how special you are.'

'Mind if I cut in?' a smooth voice drawled. Leigh turned to see the face of her mother's friend, Kirsten. She was wearing a white Chanel jacket, hair styled in a neat burgundy bob, makeup immaculate. Kirsten had always been Leigh's style icon; if she'd ever had a bad hair day, Leigh had never seen it.

Kirsten gave her a hug. 'And how's my star doing?' she asked.

'Never better.' Leigh flashed an electric smile.

'Think you might have time for an interview before you skip town? I know it's probably the last thing you want to do now you're home, but my boss would kill me if I didn't at least ask.'

'I always have time for you,' Leigh said. 'I'm busy the rest of today, but how about sometime later in the week?'

'Whatever works for you, sweetheart. Well, I'll leave you two to catch up. Enjoy your visit.'

'Oh!' Leigh said, spinning back to her mother. 'Speaking of which, I'm catching up with all my old classmates today, but I'm dying to see my other friends as well. What would you say to me having a get-together?'

Shelagh's soft green-grey eyes glowed, warm, and familiar, as she smiled at Leigh. 'Of course you can, my darling. I'll get onto it right away.'

'You're the best,' Leigh said. Then, catching the eyes of her friends, she disappeared into the crowd.

Leigh, Gabriella, and Ana spent the day reminiscing and cringing over old photos and stories from their teenage years. Some of their old classmates were jealous of their success. Others had never uttered a word to them, but relished in the moment of glory by association, soaking up any hint of the limelight they could. Most of their friends, however, just wanted to spend time with them. It had been so long since they were all together in the same room. The hours slipped away as Leigh, Gabriella and Ana sat among the group, simply enjoying each other's company.

+ + +

Leigh, radiant in summery citrus with a fresh mojito in hand, watched from the sidelines as the school hall swirled with all the glitz and glamour Champaign could muster. Despite what Marco said, she wasn't sure she would ever acclimatise to this. Gabriella and Ana, obviously both well-accustomed to the stage, were having far less difficulty. Stella McCartney had whipped up a whimsical bit of deliciousness for Ana and, as usual, Gabriella's asymmetrical style made her look irresistibly elegant.

Leigh smiled. It had been a superb day, capped with an amazing party set to continue for some time yet. Nevertheless, she could use a little air. Setting her mojito down, she quietly made her way backstage, to the spot she'd taken comfort from when she felt pressure at school: her little place of solace.

As she sat down, she heard footsteps. *Could it be him?* she wondered, her heart suddenly racing.

'Leigh? Is that you?' a voice whispered from the shadows behind her. She swivelled and looked up at the unmistakeable silhouette of Marco Carrera. He extended his hand to help her off the floor. She took it sheepishly.

'What are you doing here?' he asked.

'Taking a break from all the fuss. To be honest, I'm a little overwhelmed. I don't feel like a celebrity just yet. I'm still the same girl I was at school – the only difference is I've lost my ponytails.'

'Of course you are, but I always believed you'd be famous one day, and look, it's finally happened! I couldn't be prouder of you.'

With that, he put his arm around her. Instinctively, she nestled into the warmth of his coat.

Oh my God, is this really happening?

Confirmation followed as his warm, soft lips touched hers. She didn't resist.

'I've wanted to do that for years,' he said, in the sultry, put-on French accent she remembered so well from her drama days, before launching into another forbidden kiss. This time, she felt his hand circling the contour of her breast.

It felt so right. So tender, so passionate – unlike with Chad, who didn't waste much time on foreplay. At the thought of her boyfriend, she stilled. Reluctantly, she pulled away.

'We'd better get back. Gabriella and Ana will be looking for me by now,' she mumbled, barely hearing her own words above her pulsating heart. She rejoined the party and watched from the corner of her eye as Marco followed a full minute later, blending into the crowd as if nothing had happened.

It was only later, as people started saying their goodbyes, that he slipped a little piece of paper into her hand. Twenty excruciating minutes passed before she was able to excuse herself to the bathroom. Once there, she found a cubicle and locked the door behind her.

Legs wobbly, she leaned against the wall. The paper shook in her hands as she unfolded it to reveal the message inside. *'Meet me at 360 Degrees. One hour.'*

Chapter 3

Leigh was over Chad. Period.

The thought struck her like a slap. An ice-cold – yet somehow refreshing – slap. Her womanising, bickering boyfriend could go to hell in a handbag. How could she have only just realised this?

With a rebellious thrill, she fished out her phone and typed out a text: *'We are done, Chad Hepburn! In fact, there never was a we – just a you! And you're a dick, so you can dick off!'*

Her fingertips ghosted over the screen, ready to send it, before she shook her head and deleted the words. She put the phone aside and flopped back on her bed, letting out an exasperated sigh. The blue goose-down duvet her grandmother had made her was soft beneath her skin. Posters of Janet Evans, Amy Van Dyken and Tracy Caulkins, her idols as a young swimmer, stared down at her.

God, she felt like a teenage girl again, moping over a stupid boy. A boy who'd never even loved her in the first place, probably.

Tears started to well in her eyes. *No*, she told herself. *Stop it, Leigh. You've cried enough over that lowlife. You deserve better. You deserve...*

Her thoughts turned to Marco: considerate, amiable, and tender – so far removed from Chad's brash, intense demeanour. She wasn't one to cheat, but she just couldn't help herself. The way that Marco made her feel, the way he looked at her, the way he'd always supported her in reaching her dreams... well, how could she resist?

Oh, I hope Marco feels the same way I do. It had only been a week since they'd started to meet up in secret, but she was already completely head over heels.

The thought of pursuing something with Marco conjured a sparkle within her, a shine of anticipation. She brushed her fingertips across the duvet, casting her mind back to their very first 'official' date.

+ + +

'Oh, my goodness, Marco – 360 Degrees is packed!' Leigh had turned to her companion, quickly getting lost in his dreamy green eyes. 'I wonder if we'll have room to dance. Didn't you say you were going to teach me some erotic Latin American moves?'

Marco had gripped her hand and led her to the centre of the dance floor. 'Relax, my beautiful,' he'd whispered, lifting her and twirling her around gracefully, keeping time with the music. They'd danced for what seemed like hours.

'I'm all tuckered out. Let's savour this moment with a cocktail,' Leigh had delighted in saying.

'A pina colada this time, *mon cheri?*'

'Hell yes!' Leigh had sat down, seductively pushing her strap off her shoulder, then lifted her hair to cool down her neck as she watched him stroll to the bar. There had been no queue, the dance floor swallowing up the masses, so he was back in no time.

'Put those drinks down, you stallion,' she'd said, drawing the curtain of the Velvet Lounge. 'I've got something more appetising for you.'

'Oh, you bad girl. I'm all yours,' he'd said, as she ripped off his shirt.

It had continued like that for some time. They would catch up for coffee and spend hours chatting about everything and nothing. Marco loved listening to her talk about her adventures overseas. She regaled him with tales of breathtaking landscapes, exotic cuisines, and charming locals, as well as her progress with her training – and, of course, the shenanigans she and her cohorts had got up to since leaving school. Everything that Chad hated to hear. Not that he would even listen; the moment she started talking about anything that had to do with life outside of their little Champaign bubble, Chad would shut down.

And Marco himself had so many fascinating stories. It appears he'd been all over the country, meeting interesting people, doing so many incredible things.

'…but my favourite must be Camelback Mountain. I used to go there all the time as a boy. The view from the top, especially at sunset? Breathtaking. It's like the very heavens have opened.'

'It sounds amazing.'

'I'll have to take you sometime.'

'You certainly will,' Leigh had said, with a laugh.

Afterwards, they would disappear into the bathroom of the coffee shop, or into Marco's Lamborghini Countach, and make passionate love, over and over again. Leigh had the stamina of a swimmer, and Marco, for an older man, was quite the competitor.

Yesterday, Marco had invited Leigh to his place for drinks. It had been a perfect evening, with barely a cloud in the sky, and the warm breeze had rustled through the leaves as she'd approached the steps of his home. She'd arrived at 6.30 p.m., dressed to the nines, her long, straight chestnut hair caught in the wind. She'd waited in anticipation for him to open the front door of his Mediterranean-style home. As soon as he had, all plans of decorum had gone out the window.

'Take me while I'm hot,' she'd purred, plunging into his waiting arms as he'd rapidly started unbuttoning her blouse.

Marco's warm lips had caressed her half-undressed body, his bare chest against her skin adding to her elation. They'd guzzled down their cocktails, wasting no time before enjoying the glow of the fireplace. The softness of the rug underneath Marco had invited further ecstasy as she'd dominated top position, guiding his hand for her own personal pleasure. They'd rolled over, a collision with the baroque ornaments flanking the fireplace doing little to dampen the moment as he'd entered her ever so gently.

I've died, Leigh had thought. *I've died and gone to Heaven. This man has taken technique to the next level! Am I in for the ride of my life?*

Her fingernails had pressed into his back, gripping him tightly. He'd pounded into her, hitting all the right spots, whispering her name. Within minutes, he'd ejaculated after pulling out of her.

'I think a toast is appropriate right now. Only the best bottle of French champagne is good enough for you, Leigh,' he'd said. He'd poured the remainder of the bottle over her glistening body, licking her all over.

They'd continued for hours, with one erotic lovemaking session after another, spicing it up a little more each time. They couldn't get enough of each other. At one point, Leigh had had her legs wrapped around his torso as they'd glided into the kitchen. Marco had propped her buttocks on the counter, knocking over the condiment set. He'd continued kissing her, eagerly making his way to her breasts, down her stomach and finally circling her outer vagina. He'd inserted his middle finger to a shriek of delight from Leigh, arousing her to new heights. She'd climaxed seconds later. He'd swung her over, then penetrated her robustly for their final session of the evening.

'You're beautiful,' he'd whispered breathlessly. 'Lovely. Leigh, I think I lo–'

+   +   +

The sound of her mother calling shook Leigh from her memories. Tonight was the party her mother had organised. Bending over, she rifled through her suitcase and changed into the flowing red dress she'd gotten designed for the celebrations in Beijing after her big win. It was one of the best pieces she owned, magnificently accentuating her features, bringing out her eyes until she appeared lit from within. Marco would be there tonight; she needed to look her best.

As she descended the staircase, she saw Shelagh standing at the door, welcoming a group of guests. Skipping a few steps, she ran towards her mother and scooped her up in a big bear hug.

'Mom, I can't believe what you've put together for me! This looks amazing,' Leigh said. 'You are truly the most hospitable person in the world. Aren't we just so blessed with our gorgeous piece of suburbia? No wonder our home has always been the party capital!' Her eyes sparkled teasingly.

Their home was the perfect setting for garden parties and functions. The sunken media room, complete with a pull-out stage, overflowed with a boisterous crowd. Lights flickered across the tiles, their different hues blending harmoniously with the natural surroundings of the sandstone alfresco area. Friends were reuniting, some trying to impress by being pretentious, others slinging around derogatory wisecracks, trying to make a name for themselves. It wasn't working.

Leigh only had eyes for one man. And it wasn't the one who made terrible excuses, constantly disappeared on business trips, and never showed up when she needed him.

'Gabs, don't you think Marco's looking quite dashing tonight?' Leigh asked.

A shadowy frown furrowed Gabriella's forehead. 'I guess? I mean, to me, he's still our teacher. I know he says to call him by his name, but I always feel a little weird about it.' She looked at Leigh more closely. 'What's this all about, anyway? Has our Leigh got a little crush?'

'Oh, don't mind me. I'm just thinking out loud,' Leigh said quickly. 'I must make the rounds. I'll see you in a bit.' She wound her way through the party, chatting with everyone she passed. Throughout the years, she'd accumulated a large following of friends. People seemed to gravitate towards her.

'Leigh!'

She heard someone calling her name over the loud music and babble. Turning to see a tall man with short dark hair and a well-trimmed beard, she flashed him a dazzling smile.

Craig Ryan was a lieutenant with the Champaign Police Department. He was a close friend of the family, the father of one of Leigh's closest friends, and had known her since she was in swim diapers.

'I just wanted to tell you how proud I am,' he said. 'You've done amazingly well for yourself, Leigh, and I hope you know that we're all behind you, one hundred percent.'

'Thanks, Uncle Craig,' she said. 'It means a lot. But how are you? Have you been taking care of yourself?'

'You shouldn't be worrying about me, sweetheart. But yes, I'm getting all my fruits and veggies. I'm even down to smoking just one pack a day.'

She shook her head; she knew he was a hopeless case. 'And how's Chelsea?' she asked. 'It's been ages since we've talked.'

'She's doing great. She's working at the Olympic Coast National Marine Sanctuary right now. Little less tropical than she'd prefer, but she loves the work.'

'That's fantastic,' Leigh said. 'Send her lots of love from me.'

'I will. I can't seem to find your mother, so please thank her for an awesome party on my behalf.'

'Aw, are you leaving already?'

'Early shift tomorrow,' he said, shrugging. 'Someone has to make sure the precinct doesn't burn down, even on a Saturday.'

'Well, we all thank you for your service.' She gave a mock salute, and he chuckled.

'Don't get too cheeky with me now, girl. You go enjoy the party – you deserve to have a little fun.'

As Craig pushed his way through the throngs of people, a call stopped him in his tracks.

'Well, ain't you a sight for sore eyes,' drawled the voice, its Southern twang unmistakeable. 'Craig Ryan. It's been a dog's age.'

'Kirsten Wells.' He turned around, sporting a wide grin. 'Lovely as always. You know how busy I get down at the station.'

'I certainly don't miss it,' she said. Craig raised an eyebrow. 'Well, just a little bit. But the pay is better at the *Chronicle* and WCIA, and you know how I like the finer things!' She ran a finger down Craig's chest.

'I saw the big piece you did on Champaign's one hundredth anniversary. You're moving up in the world, huh? Got your own little regular time slot?'

'What can I say? The camera loves me!'

'You certainly have a gift for it,' Craig nodded.

'You're gonna make me blush.' She lightly smacked him on the shoulder. 'Although... I have been getting bored lately. If you've got any cases lying around that need an expert eye, send them my way, will you?'

He agreed and went on his way, while Kirsten spun on her stilettos to find Shelagh.

Leigh had seen and spoken to everyone she'd planned to.

'Leigh!' Gabriella squealed, tipping slightly as she walked Leigh's way. 'I'm heading out, but I wanted to see your face before I left. Sorry to be leaving so soon – Mama's got a full day planned out for the two of us. You know how she is.'

The two girls broke into fits of laughter. Suddenly, Gabriella paled.

'What is it, Gabs?'

'I just... I thought I saw someone.'

'Who?'

'It's nothing,' she said, with a smile. 'Probably just a little too much to drink. Anyhoo, I must go. I'll call you tomorrow, yeah? Maybe we can do dinner. Mama would love to have you over. Enjoy the rest of your evening.' With a kiss to Leigh's cheek, she was gone.

As Leigh shuffled through the crowd of people, she collided with a skinny man with dark hair and an unkempt beard, nearly knocking him over.

'Oh, pardon me,' Leigh said. The man looked familiar, but she couldn't quite place him. 'I'm so sorry! I didn't mean to–'

'Don't worry about it,' he said, his voice low. 'It's all good.'

A little while later, Leigh received a call and disappeared into the darkness of the night.

+   +   +

Alan had the perfect physique for a long-distance runner: he was medium height, with a light frame and slim legs. He was on his morning run, training for his next marathon on the outskirts of Champaign, when he noticed something strange out of the corner of his eye.

He stopped mid-stride, then doubled back, looking down from the edge of the bridge into the ravine below. He saw something large lying half-submerged in the running water. Frowning, he craned his neck, unsure exactly what he was witnessing.

Against his better judgment, Alan decided to take a closer look. He made his way slowly down the steep-sided valley of the ravine, careful not to hurt his ankles. As he approached it, and began to suspect what it was, he instinctively wanted to turn around and run. However, compassion made him step closer.

He leaned over the purple rug and saw human hair cascading from it.

It was a body.

Immediately, Alan took out his phone and called 911, his eyes fixed on the long, beautiful hair spread across the woman's deathly pale face.

Chapter 4

Even early on a Saturday morning, it was mayhem at the police station.

'Craig! I need you in my office, now!' ordered the South African-born Chief of Police, Riaan Gietersan, as he slammed down his phone. Craig immediately headed into his office.

'What's up, Chief?' he asked.

'A homicide has just been reported.'

'Really? *Here?*'

Riaan shook his head. 'Here are the coordinates. Find out what happened and get the bastard. Take whomever you need.'

At the crime scene, Craig acknowledged Alan's statement, dismissed him, and advised him to remain available for further questioning. A few moments later, his backup team arrived, trailed by the team of forensic detectives.

'I've cordoned off the area. Make sure no one crosses the line,' Craig ordered. He shook his head. 'For fuck's sake, I thought I'd left this type of shit behind in Chicago.'

He'd certainly seen his fair share of corpses in his eleven-year stint as a senior detective in the Chicago Police Department. There was a reason he'd left the bigger city and returned to his hometown.

'This is Champaign's first homicide in fifty years, isn't it?' blurted Officer Cody Waterman. His brand-new silver badge glimmered in the sunlight, blinding all his more seasoned colleagues in the Homicide Division.

Craig bent down to uncover the body, gently sweeping the hair off her face with gloved hands. He recognised her instantly. Startled, he stood up.

'It can't be!' he said. He was frozen. Shaken. He couldn't stop the tremor that was making its way through his limbs. 'No. Oh my God, no. Leigh... It's Leigh O'Rielly!'

How will I break this to Dylan and Shelagh?

Craig inhaled deeply to compose himself, then started issuing orders. While the forensic detectives bagged items of possible interest, taking samples of everything around them, the coroner, Dr Barry Blake, checked over the partially undressed body. He instantly observed marks of ligature strangulation around the full circumference of her neck, from something thin, like a scarf or a length of wire. There were multiple deep stab wounds on her chest and abdomen, along with several more superficial cuts. Red bands on her wrists and legs were evidence she'd been bound.

How Goddamn callous, Barry thought.

And with that, he officially pronounced Leigh dead.

+ + +

This is going to kill them, Craig thought. *Why me? Why the hell did I insist it be me?*

Of course, he knew why. It had been to soften the blow. As if this blow could ever be softened! Wrap it, pack it, ship it any way he liked – it would still kill them.

Dry orange leaves crunched under his feet as he pulled up his coat collar. He pressed the doorbell of the O'Riellys' luxurious home. Just yesterday, he'd been here, celebrating. Leigh had been so happy. So alive.

He remembered the first time he'd visited this home with his daughter. Chelsea and Leigh had been swimming together since elementary school; with practices and playdates, they'd spent a lot of time in each other's pockets.

My poor Chels... shit. How am I going to break this to you?

His thoughts were interrupted as the door opened. The fall sun lit up the huge smile on Shelagh O'Rielly's face. She was a graceful woman, for whom decorum always remained the order of the day. Her celestial beauty interlocked with her elegant and cultured manner. She had brown hair with mahogany undertones, and a fair complexion, a remnant of her Irish heritage.

'Good morning, Craig. To what do I owe the honour of your unexpected yet welcome visit?' she asked playfully, her eyes twinkling.

Keeping his voice solemn, he replied, 'Shelagh, is Dylan home?'

'Funny you should ask. He's just about to leave for New York – I was helping him pack his last few items. Please do come in and take a seat. I'll call him down.'

She showed him through the elegant white entrance hall, which was adorned with classical sculptures, then into the living room. As she ascended the imposing staircase, calling for her husband, Craig steeled himself for what was to come.

They returned moments later. Judging from their faces, it was clear they'd picked up on his sombre mood.

'Craig, what's wrong?' Dylan asked. 'What's happened?'

'I'm sorry. I'm so sorry. Leigh... she was found down by the ravine this morning. Someone...'

'No,' Shelagh choked out.

'I'm sorry, Shel. Leigh's... no longer with us.'

A deathly silence followed. For that split second, it felt as if the world had come to a standstill. Then, in unison, Dylan and Shelagh burst into tears and hugged each other. Craig stepped back, placing a hand on Dylan's shoulder. Clearly, he was trying desperately to maintain his strength for Shelagh, who was, by now, totally, and utterly inconsolable.

'What insane creature would do this?' she screamed through her tears, clutching at her heart.

Craig squeezed Dylan's shoulder. 'We're gonna get this guy, and we'll make him pay. I promise you.'

'Bullshit!' Dylan yelled. 'Murdered? I don't believe it! She was in this house just last night. How do you know it was her?'

'It was her,' Craig said, his voice barely above a whisper. 'I'm so sorry, Dylan. But it was her.'

A moment passed between them all, filled with sobs and ragged breaths.

'Craig,' Dylan hissed. 'I want you to nail this bastard. Don't give up until you find him.' He lightly stroked the curve of Shelagh's cheek, then helped her to sit down on the couch, before turning back to Craig. 'Please excuse me. I... I must call in to the office.'

Swiftly, he walked away down the hall, no doubt to let the floodgates down fully. He'd always been a private person, but Craig hoped he wouldn't keep his grief hidden away. Craig had seen too many people destroyed by the loss of a loved one; the last thing he wanted was for this to happen to Dylan.

Shelagh curled up on the couch, eyes puffy, face glazed, still breathing harshly. Craig sat beside her, sharing her tears in silence. Good old friends didn't need to say a word.

+ + +

In the morgue, Dylan bent over and tenderly kissed his daughter on the forehead, his eyes flowing with tears. Flashbacks of her life streamed through his mind.

'You were an absolute joy to your mother and I, my darling princess,' he whispered. 'Who did this to you? Who would take you from us in such a reprehensible manner? How are we going to live without you?'

Shelagh sat in the waiting area with Craig by her side. She hadn't been able to bear the thought of seeing her daughter in this state, so Dylan had gone in to identify the body alone.

By midday on Saturday, the formalities were finalised, and Leigh's body was transported to the coroner. Barry attributed the death to strangulation, estimating that it had occurred six to eight hours prior to the discovery of her body. There were thirty-five stab wounds on her torso, and ligature marks on her wrists and legs, indicating she may have been sexually assaulted; however, there was no trace of semen.

That wasn't the strangest thing Barry found, though. Upon shifting her hair to examine her neck, he discovered something that made his blood run cold.

'Good God, as if I hadn't seen it all this morning,' he cursed.

For a moment, he and his assistant stood in enigmatic silence. Then, with all the authority he could muster, he spoke. 'Get Lieutenant Ryan on the phone. I don't think we're dealing with a random killing here. This puts everything into another dimension.'

Craig arrived shortly after. Barry pointed to the lobe of Leigh's left ear, which had been roughly sawn off.

'Shit,' Craig said.

'Do you think this could be a signature?' Barry asked.

'I've never seen this before, but it could be. I'll get my detectives to step up their investigations and run the rap sheets of every felon in this state. Those fucking loser parolees aren't exempt from this one, either. Jesus, the

list of suspects is going to be five fucking miles long...' He shook his head, furrowing his brows.

Chad Hepburn, that little shitface boyfriend of Leigh's, could even be top of the pops. Asshole had been cheating on her for years. Craig didn't know what she'd ever seen in him.

Time to question the little chop, he thought. *He better have some answers.*

Chapter 5

Whistling, Chad walked into the station on Sunday morning, swinging his designer jacket over his shoulder. As he sat down in the interrogation room and made himself comfortable, he looked straight into Lieutenant Craig Ryan's steely eyes.

Craig took a deep breath before diving in. 'Alright,' he said. 'Let's get straight to the point. Where were you on the night of Friday June 10th, between 10 p.m. and 2 a.m.?'

Chad shifted in his seat. 'I'd just flown in from San Francisco. I was there for a week on business,' he said, shoulders back, a smirk on his face. 'I went straight to my office to tie up a few things and got waylaid with reports and emails. I was exhausted from my trip but had to prepare for my 8 a.m. meeting the following morning. I fell asleep in my chair and woke up at 5.30 a.m., totally disorientated. After going home to shower, I returned to the office at 7 a.m., passing Starbucks on the way to pick up a caffe mocha. There's no question that chocolate and coffee are flavours meant for each other, right?'

Craig merely growled.

'Right,' Chad continued. 'Anyway, Leigh's mother called me later that morning and told me the horrific news. I immediately left the office to be with them. So, Lieutenant, there you have it. All my moves that day are accounted for. Leigh was the love of my life. Everyone, including you, knows that!' His voice wobbled at the end of his speech, yet still, a brave touch of defiance slithered through.

Craig mulled over whether it was grief or show. Chad had been a star drama student, after all, though

Craig suspected it was only so he could crawl his way into Leigh's heart.

Regardless, Craig didn't believe a word this little shit was saying. His body language spelt out a different story, and over the years, Craig had developed a strong prejudice against him. Thanks to regular get-togethers at the O'Riellys' and Shelagh's vocal disapproval, Craig had seen and heard about all the shit he'd pulled. The way he treated Leigh – *had* treated Leigh – was frankly inexcusable. Craig had even told him so on several occasions, straight to his face, although that was usually after quite a few drinks.

Still, as difficult as it was, Craig had to put those personal feelings aside to steer this investigation in a professional and ethical manner.

'What proof do I have that you went straight to your office, Chad? Any witnesses?'

'Well, actually... there was one.'

'Oh, really? And who may that be?'

Clearly uncomfortable, Chad cleared his throat. 'Georgia. Georgia was there.'

'Who the hell is Georgia?'

'She's my secretary,' Chad mumbled, scrutinising the parquet flooring below his feet.

'And what exactly was she doing at the office – after hours, even – when you were on a business trip?'

'She was… waiting for me.'

'Ah-ha,' Craig snapped. 'So, you *did* have a motive to get rid of Leigh. That poor girl was in the way of your relationship with your secretary, wasn't she?'

'No, no, Lieutenant – you've got it all wrong. I loved Leigh. I told you she was the love of my life. I would never do anything to harm her!'

'Then why was Georgia waiting for you if you were so in love with Leigh? Spell it out for me, boy. I'm waiting.'

'Well, I… I had a bit of a fling with Georgia. It was nothing serious, just… you know.'

'Know *what?*' Craig demanded, banging his fist on the table.

'It was just fun! Just one of those office affairs.'

Craig scoffed. 'Don't you know you're playing with fire, dipping your pen into company ink?'

'She made a play for me first! What hot-blooded male would say no?' Defensively, Chad crossed his arms. 'Alright, so I used her! There's nothing wrong with that, is there? I wasn't married, I knew nothing would ever come of it, and she knew about my relationship with Leigh. It was a fling, for shit's sake!'

'Did Leigh know?'

Chad deflated. 'I think she knew that something was going on, but she never said... no, I don't think she knew about Georgia.'

'So, what time did Georgia leave the office?'

'Maybe around 1 a.m.? I'm not too sure. As I told you, Lieutenant, I was tired and fell asleep in my chair.'

Great. Another suspect to add to the list.

'Okay, Chad. We'll call this a day, but don't even think of stepping a foot out of Champaign. You're going to be called in for more questioning, so we need you to be available. Have I made myself clear?'

'Yes, but please don't mention Georgia to Leigh's parents. It would just hurt them more, and we're finally on good terms.' He sniffed. 'Ironic, huh?'

At the door, Chad paused for a moment, before turning back to Craig. 'I'm no killer, Lieutenant. I would never hurt Leigh. I hope you find the person who did.'

Chapter 6

Kirsten breezed out of the WCIA station building, heading for her car. She was a part-time reporter there with a regular segment, along with her duties at the *Chronicle*. CBS was running a special on Leigh and had reached out to Kirsten to host. It would be a celebration of Leigh's life and achievements, ending with a plea to anyone with information on her death to contact the police department. Kirsten needed to be on air in less than two hours, but she still had time to visit an old friend.

Prior to beginning her journalism career, she'd been a detective with the New York Police Department, and a long stint in Chicago, where she and Craig had been partners. Eleven years they'd worked together, solving cases, sharing gut instincts; they were each other's yin and yang. Even now, Craig would often pick her brain on challenging cases. She had fond memories of her carefree days as Craig's high school sweetheart and cherished the close friendship they still held.

Kirsten turned her convertible towards the precinct. On her way there, she thought more about Leigh. Tears streamed down her face as she recollected the numerous interviews she'd conducted with Leigh over the years, and the magnificent time she'd spent with Dylan and Shelagh in Beijing, witnessing Leigh's greatest accomplishment. Kirsten had been so proud of her.

This murder is personal, she thought, wiping her cheeks. *I'll insist that Craig involve me in this investigation. If it's the last thing I do, I'll help him find this killer, just like old times.*

She'd never had children herself and never intended to – a choice she didn't regret, as she'd told many a bewildered suitor in days gone by – but Leigh had become like a daughter to her over the years. Kirsten had watched her grow up, had taken her to swim practices and competitions and spoiled her with the latest style of swimsuits every single year for her birthday.

'You can have both function and fashion, darling,' she would say to the wide-eyed girl. 'You're doing great out there – you should look the part as well.'

Leigh had been such a loving, free spirit... popular, too. God had she been popular. Especially with the boys! Kirsten couldn't help but smile at the thought of Leigh's wildly vocal male fan base. She could've had any one of them without batting an eyelid.

So much like me, Kirsten thought, then laughed aloud. *In your dreams, Ms Wells. Leigh had ten times the talent and twenty times the discipline you ever did!*

While Kirsten had helped shape Leigh's career, had raised funds for her, opened doors for her, championed her every move, there was no question the glory belonged to Leigh and Leigh alone. First had come the medals – only silvers and golds, mind you – then the endorsements, thick and fast. Nike, Adidas, Red Bull. Even Wonderbra, for frig's sake. Of course, Leigh's poster girl looks had played a part. No doubt about *that*. But dammit, she'd been good. Hell, she'd been incredible!

And, best of all, she'd been oblivious to it all. At heart, she'd been a simple, genuine girl with a disposition so sunny it could've melted the Arctic.

Kirsten wished Leigh was still in Melbourne; this wouldn't have happened. It was a crying shame to have lost such a beautiful soul.

A solitary tear rolled down Kirsten's cheek as she pulled into the car park of the Champaign PD, right next to Craig's car. She was barely through the door of his office before she started to speak. 'Craig, what do you have for me? Let's bring this bastard down!'

Craig put the sheaf of files he'd been studying down on his desk. 'Seriously, Kirsten?'

'Hey, cowboy, just because you're not allowed to say it doesn't mean you can't.'

He sat back and scowled at her.

'Listen, Leigh was just as important to me as she was to you,' Kirsten continued, her eyes blazing. 'I can be your eyes and ears out there. Have you forgotten all the crimes we've solved together over the years? I may not be a detective anymore, but I've still got the instinct. Not to mention I have significant connections within this community.'

'Is that right? Champaign's very own belle of the ball, are we?'

'Oh, shut up, Craig. Be serious now. I'm not taking no for an answer; whether you like it or not, I'm getting involved in this investigation. So, dear heart, am I on your team or not?' She flicked her head to the side, sweeping her hair back over her forehead.

Craig knew Kirsten well enough to be aware that when she set her sights on something, she never let it go.

Maybe she could be an adroit negotiator, unofficially assisting him. He was fully aware of the consequences of crossing ethical lines with her on his team; however, he knew he could trust her and believed she could be a superb ally.

'Alright,' he said, finally. 'What have you picked up on all your excursions around town?'

'Well, for starters, Chad wasn't the faithful boyfriend he professes to be.'

'Tell me news, not history,' Craig scoffed. 'He confessed earlier today to an office fling.'

'With Georgia?' she asked, raising one eyebrow.

'Yes. Trust me, I've given this a lot of thought, and quite honestly, I don't think that little prick is capable of murder. He's too weak and self-important. All he's worried about is when he'll get his next lay.' He rolled his eyes. 'He is, plain and simple, the proverbial gigolo – and way too stupid to have not left any evidence at the crime scene. We're dealing with a professional killer here, Kirst. I feel it in my bones. The perp is someone who's done this before.' He paused, frowning. 'Wait, how do you know about Georgia?'

'I told you I'm connected,' she said, holding her hands in the air.

'Okay, enough of this bullshit banter. Answer my question, Kirsten.'

'Well, my source told me Georgia is, in fact, not the only one,' Kirsten replied, strutting across the room. 'I've stumbled upon numerous names; it looks like a Girl Guide registry list!'

'I need all those names. Maybe his alibi isn't so airtight after all.' Grimacing, Craig rubbed at his neck. 'I still haven't come across anyone with a vendetta against Leigh, or who displayed acrimonious behaviour towards her.' He stood and gave himself an impromptu neck adjustment. 'Ah, that feels better. Kirst, remember one thing: the evidence so far is pointing to a professional, not some petty little thief-turned-killer. This is just like those horrific incidents in Riverdale and Washington Park.

Believe me, partner, we haven't scratched the surface of this investigation yet.'

Always the gentleman, Craig walked Kirsten to her car and, as she pressed the remote to open her door, playfully smacked her on the buttocks. With a twinkle in his eye, he said, 'Fit, forty and firm!'

She flicked her immaculate locks. 'You can only wish, buck!'

She sped off to be back to the station in time for hair and make-up. As he walked inside, Craig called Georgia to come in for questioning.

This is going to be an interesting sound out, he thought. *I have a feeling I'm going to get more than I've bargained for.*

Chapter 7

Craig had just extinguished his cigarette when he looked up and saw an extremely attractive young lady enter the precinct, swaying her hips as if in time to music. Her voluptuous pout turned heads. He had to wonder if it was real, or if she was another dermal filler devotee. The younger male officers fell over each other to assist her, eagerly escorting her into the interrogation room, so Craig knew she could only be Georgia Thornton.

Entering the room, he slammed the door behind him, adjusting the light to make it brighter. 'Right then, Georgia: where were you on the night of Friday June 10th between 10 p.m. and 2 a.m.?' Pulling out a federally issued chair, he casually placed his foot on the seat. He leaned over, resting his arm on his leg.

She went on to give the same story as Chad, virtually in verbatim. That immediately raised alarm bells, as it could've been rehearsed. Craig monitored her every move. Her every word. His brain turned into a one-armed bandit. As the interrogation progressed, she became less forthright than Chad, her answers increasingly evasive.

This girl's holding back, Craig thought, huffing out a sigh. *She thinks she's being clever, hmm? It's time to start turning the screws.*

He stared intently at Georgia, trying to gauge her reaction.

'So, you're saying you had nothing to do with Leigh's death?' he asked, his voice sharp and suspicious.

Georgia shook her head vehemently. 'No, of course not,' she said. 'Why would I?'

After studying her face for a moment longer, Craig removed his foot from the chair, sighing. 'Well, I'll be honest with you. We have reason to believe that you and Chad were both involved in Leigh's murder.'

Georgia's eyes widened. 'Chad?' she said, her voice rising. 'Why would he have anything to do with this?'

Craig leaned forward, his eyes narrowing.

'Because he was involved with Leigh,' he said. 'And we know you have strong feelings for him. It's not a stretch to imagine you might've wanted to get rid of Leigh so you could have him all to yourself.'

Georgia's cheeks turned red. 'That's ridiculous,' she spat. 'I had nothing to do with Leigh's death. And as for Chad, he can take care of himself. I don't need to kill anyone to win his affection.'

Craig decided to try another angle. The entry points of the stab wounds indicated the killer was left-handed, so he asked Georgia to write down the names of all the other women in the office. To his dismay, she picked up the pen with her right hand.

Could be ambidextrous. Or maybe she's trying to throw us off her scent.

As he watched her write, he noticed the smirk on her face. 'What's so amusing?'

'Nothing, Lieutenant Ryan. I was just thinking that Chad's reputation will be tarnished after this. He's been a very busy boy, you know! It's time to introduce Macy and add her to the mix. I must warn you, though – she's not the type to sit back and take the rap for anyone else.'

'Macy?' Craig grunted. That was a new name. 'Where does she fit into the picture?'

Georgia fidgeted. 'Well,' she said, shrugging and avoiding eye contact with Craig, 'I thought you already knew. Why else would I be here?'

'Because you killed your lover's girlfriend.'

She scoffed. 'Please.'

'Illuminate me, then.'

She hesitated. 'Where do I start?'

'How about from the beginning?'

'Um, you see… Macy and I often had threesomes with Chad. Usually after a long day at work. She was also at the office that night, and she left just after me.'

Every hue of the rainbow decked Georgia's complexion. 'How embarrassing,' she mumbled under her breath, tugging on her miniskirt. She raised her head, her mood a little more upbeat. 'So, you see, Lieutenant, that clears me.'

Has a red herring just been cast?

'I'll be the one to determine who's guilty or not, Georgia. You leave the police work to me. Now, is there anything more you're withholding? Bear in mind, I *will* get to the bottom of all your office shenanigans, with or without your assistance.'

'No.' She quickly shook her head. 'Nothing more from my side.' Her piercing blue eyes held a bold challenge as she added, 'Talk to Macy. She may have more information for you.'

'Alright, then,' Craig said, rolling up his sleeves. 'That'll be all for now. Thank you for your co-operation. Don't go anywhere, my girl; you may be required to come in again for further questioning.'

'Of course, Lieutenant.'

And with that, she was gone. Craig ordered Cody to put her under surveillance, then made a call to one Macy Mulligan – a sales representative who worked for the same company as Chad and Georgia – instructing her to come down to the station the following morning.

Craig sat at his desk and stared at the file in front of him. Chad's name was circled, highlighted, and underlined multiple times. Craig couldn't shake the feeling that he'd overlooked something crucial in the initial investigation. He had moved on to other suspects and other leads, but Chad remained in the back of his mind. And now, with the involvement of Georgia and Macy, Chad had clear motive to commit the crime. The spotlight was back on him.

Craig rubbed his eyes and took a deep breath, trying to clear his mind. This was a high-profile case, and he couldn't afford to make any mistakes. The pressure was mounting, and the thought of making any misstep made him break out in a cold sweat. He knew that Chad was a slippery character. If Chad *was* the one behind the heinous crime, he would do everything in his power to prove it.

With a renewed sense of purpose, Craig dived back into the case file, examining every detail with fresh eyes. He pored over witness statements, studied the forensics reports, and re-examined all the evidence collected at the scene of the crime. As the hours passed, he found himself getting more and more suspicious of Chad. He would work day and night to make sure that justice was served. Nothing could be left to chance, and every stone needed to be overturned.

Craig closed his eyes for a moment. The game was afoot once again, and he was ready to play it. He would find the answers he needed, no matter the cost.

Chapter 8

With unrelenting thoroughness, the forensic detective team combed through the area of bush and scrub where Leigh's body had been located. Late on Sunday afternoon, Randy Brightman, a forensic veteran, stumbled on a roll of duct tape. His eyes widened as he crouched down and saw carpet fibres stuck to the tape.

'We may have a breakthrough!' he shouted, bagging the evidence.

A few yards away, Cody was raking through the barren soil, and noticed something shining through the top layer. 'This looks like a button,' he said. He picked it up and dropped it again; his latex gloves were slippery from his sweaty hands. 'Could this be a connection, Deputy?'

'Bag it,' Randy said. 'We'll send these to the lab for testing.'

Minutes later, Craig stepped out of his vehicle and made his way down to the ravine. 'Got anything yet, guys?' he bellowed. 'Don't stop until we've found every piece of evidence. I want this bastard to swing for this!'

As he entered the implement-filled tent, he instantly spotted the two evidence bags, standing proudly on the table. 'Finally, we've got something to fucking work with! Well done. Cody, take these down to the lab, will you? Have you left yet?'

Head spinning, Cody quivered in his boots, still not sure how to take this man or his sarcasm.

'Any tyre or similar tracks found?' Craig asked. 'Shoe prints?'

'No,' Randy answered in a despondent tone. 'We're still looking.'

As the sun set, they decided to wrap it up for the day. 'We'll resume at 7 a.m. tomorrow, team. Thank you all for your hard work and diligence.' Craig's authoritative words landed on happy, yet tired, ears.

The team had established that it would've been impossible for a woman of Georgia's petite stature to carry a body down that steep embankment. She only weighed forty-two kilograms herself, and Leigh was heavier than that. So – for now, at least – she was placed on the board as an unlikely person of interest.

Unbeknown to the forensic team, a shadowy figure stood next to his hired car on the shoulder of the road, way above where they were working, watching their every move. This was the perfect vantage point for him to keep abreast of what was happening.

'Oh, how I love this control, this peace of mind,' he whispered. 'Rip, you are pure genius. Like you always say, no one is exempt from your clutches.'

From where he stood, no one could see him on that quiet road, the old road into the city. Licentious and luxurious in his manners, cultured and Catholic in his tastes, he united in his person the most diverse qualities of evil and destruction. To an outsider, he would've appeared as confident and fresh as a man just starting a mission after a good night's sleep. That was, at least, until he witnessed that shiny thing, they were all fussing over.

What the hell is that? He racked his brain, trying to remember what Leigh had been wearing that night.

'Nah… too far from where I dumped the bitch,' he said. He lifted his hand to his mouth, curling his finger over his lips, holding his breath for a split second.

If I recall correctly, everything was intact when I put her into the trunk. The gloves stayed on my hands throughout. I only pulled them off when I got into the car. There were no slip-ups – I'm sure of that. Why am I even stressing about this?

'Anyway,' he said, 'I've seen what I need to for now. I'd rather go back home and do something constructive. Methinks my photo collage needs an update.'

He clapped his hands together, a darkly delighted glint in his eye. 'Oops, almost forgot! I'd better buy more newspapers. Craig's love letter won't be complete without them.'

Chapter 9

The following morning, Macy Mulligan rushed into the police station at 8 a.m. sharp.

'I'm here to see Lieutenant Ryan,' she announced to the young sergeant at the front desk. He immediately got up, escorting her to the interrogation room.

Watching from his desk, Craig drank his morning coffee and decided to let her sit and hopefully sweat for a while. She wasn't as attractive as Georgia, but this little bombshell had a killer body with massive boobs. The men loved her.

As Craig walked towards the interrogation room, he saw her frantically texting. He stopped to watch her through the open door, as her phone rang, and she answered it immediately.

'Morning. Wow, this is one for the books! I know the early bird catches the worm, but aren't you pushing it a little? I'm at the police station, remember? I can't flippin' talk to you now, you goofball!'

She paused for a moment as the person on the other end spoke, then huffed, rolling her eyes.

'Yes, I'm not as ditzy as you think. Remember, my blonde hair comes from a bottle, you chauvinist pig. Oh, someone's here. *Au revoir,*' she said, her words fading into a whisper.

Craig entered the room, almost taking the door off its hinges. 'Macy, I take it? Good morning. I'm Lieutenant Craig Ryan.'

'Good morning, Lieutenant Ryan. How are you this bright and sunny morning?' she asked, scratching her forehead.

'I've been better, my girl, but I didn't ask you to come down here for the weather forecast. I need you to tell me where you were on the night of June 10th between 10 p.m. and 2 a.m.'

She leaned slightly closer to him, pursing her lips. 'I think you already know where I was, Lieutenant. Need me to refresh your memory? I was at the office that evening.'

'Why were you at the office that late, Macy?'

'Well… I was working, of course.'

'Really?' Craig snapped. 'What were you working on – the anatomies of men and women? Cut the crap and answer my question. *What* were you doing that night?'

She sucked in a breath before muttering her answer. 'Fine. I was with Chad and Georgia.'

'Go on.'

'After Chad called from the airport, Georgia and I went to the bathroom at the office and changed from our working attire into the sexy new lingerie we'd purchased at lunch that day. We were so excited to dress up for Chad.

You wouldn't understand, Lieutenant; when we found the perfect ensembles for him, with matching suspenders in red and black, we thought we'd hit the jackpot. Chad loves red and black lingerie. Ahem… we do as well! We touched up our make-up, accentuated various features, and put on our false eyelashes. I also added a Marilyn Monroe beauty spot, just here.' She put her finger to her face. The glint in her eye told Craig that she was reliving the night.

'We returned to his office and anxiously awaited his arrival for our much-anticipated soiree. Georgia draped her body over the armrest of his chair. One leg rested on the floor, the other raised onto the open drawer. She looked so sexy and seductive; I couldn't resist it any longer and started kissing her from her thighs all the way up her body 'til I reached her perfectly painted full red lips. It was orgasmic. She swung one leg over me and pulled me onto the chair. Damn, at that crucial moment, we heard the elevator open. We quickly resumed our positions – albeit reluctantly, I might add. Lieutenant, may

I have a glass of water? My throat has suddenly become quite dry.' Macy rubbed her neck.

'Sure,' Craig said, walking to the water dispenser. 'Carry on, Macy. I'm all ears.'

'Okay,' Macy said. 'The way we'd positioned ourselves on his desk would've been artistic inspiration for any sculptor. I think I could make the perfect muse.'

She giggled. Noting the look on Craig's face, she dropped the glee. 'Right. Business. A few moments later, we heard his office door open. He switched on the lights, stopped in his tracks, and just stared at us both. His briefcase fell to the floor. He removed his jacket and loosened his tie as he walked towards us. His eyes flashed with a bright sparkle, lighting up his smile – which, I have to say, was the biggest smile I've ever seen.' She paused, her tiny grin returning.

'Macy?'

'Oh! Sorry. So then,' Chad said, '*Has a page from the* Kama Sutra *come to life?* The three of us were soon engaged in all sorts of positions, each satisfying the other.

We made passionate love for hours, totally uninhibited. Chad had surprised us with new sex toys he bought on his trip. Phew, that's about all I can tell you, Lieutenant, without going into every move we made.' She seemed quite out of breath as she ran her fingers through her platinum-blonde hair.

Not to let his male side down, Craig found himself a tad aroused after hearing this amorous version of events. From the way Macy smirked, she knew it too. Still, he'd been in the game too long to let something like this break his concentration.

'What time did you leave the office, Macy?'

'I'm not sure.' She looked up at the ceiling as if trying to remember. 'I didn't look at my watch, but our rendezvous usually last about three hours. Then Chad and I had another steamy session on our own after Georgia left, so... I guess it was probably around 2?'

'So, you had plenty of time to discard the body of the woman standing in the way of your sensual lovemaking and marathon sessions at the office.'

'Absolutely not, Lieutenant! I'm simply not capable of violence.' She raised an eyebrow, lowered her voice, and gave him a coquettish glance. 'After all, I'm a lover, not a fighter.'

Cheeky little bitch. It's time to rattle her.

He changed his pace. 'Okay, Macy, I have one more question. Who were you speaking to before I walked into the room?'

After a long moment, she replied in a soft, timid voice. 'It was my mother.'

'Don't lie to me. I saw the panic on your face when you answered that call. Are you obstructing this investigation? You know I could put you away for that, don't you?'

She lowered her head, peering up from under her eyebrows. 'It was Chad.'

Chapter 10

By Tuesday morning, Craig decided he needed to speak to Gabriella and Anastasia to get a better take on Leigh's relationship with Chad. His mind was a bubbling cauldron of mystifying thoughts and theories. How many solutions were there to this puzzle? Every day, there was another fucking headline.

I'll call Gabriella first, he thought. *The Cantrellos are seriously warm and accommodating. Nothing quite beats the European charm.*

The Cantrellos' ornate home was adorned with classical flourishes. The external columns were capped with typical cyma reversa mouldings, the garden complete with statues. Michelangelo would've been so proud! The fountain was the focal point, in pride of place halfway up the garden path lined with trees and finely trimmed shrubs. Over-the-top was probably an understatement. No wonder the home was known as 'Napoli on the Hill'.

Gabriella's father, Pepe Cantrello, answered the door. He was a robust man in his late sixties with a thick Italian accent. He was Neapolitan and proud of it.

'Good morning, Lieutenant,' he said. 'Please, coming in, please. Gabriella, she come five minute. She go to store for Mama.'

As Lieutenant Ryan and Pepe sat down in the living room, the silence was broken by an extremely loud voice booming in Italian from another room. Pepe's beaming grin was a great substitute for words, yet he felt compelled to enlighten Craig.

'Ah, nothing important. My wife tell me espresso for you, yes! Please excuse.' He trundled out of the room. At the apex of awkwardness, Craig's cell phone rang.

'Speak to me,' he barked down the phone.

'It's Cody.'

'I know it's you, moron. Ever heard of caller ID?'

'Lieutenant, an envelope addressed to you just arrived at the station. It isn't an official document. This one is weird, Lieut. I don't know how the hell it got here – there's no address or zip code from the sender. Would you like me to bring it to you?'

From the sound of it, Cody was already frantically pacing the tiled floors of the precinct.

'Cody, relax. I shouldn't be much longer – maybe an hour at the most. Cheers.' He hung up.

Mind ticking into overtime, Craig stood up to look at the scores of photographs on the mantelpiece. Each one made a statement in lavish frames. The Cantrello children dominated the pictures, which ranged from their formative years to adulthood, showcasing the important milestones of their lives. The only familiar faces were in a stunning group photograph of Leigh, Gabriella, Anastasia and their favourite teacher, Mr Carrera, on the day of their graduation from Brentwood Park High. Their smiles illustrated the absolute joy of the moment.

His train of thought was interrupted by the sound of rattling cups, as Pepe returned with a tray of coffee. 'Sugar, yes?'

'One, please, Mr Cantrello. Thank you.' His long-awaited sip was interrupted by the bustle of shopping bags, car keys and a ringing cell phone, which overrode the question Pepe asked about the previous evening's football game.

'Good day, Lieutenant,' Gabriella said, as she popped her head into the living room. 'I'll be with you in a moment. Mom just needs these ingredients to finish the lasagne for lunch. I'll be right back.'

'No rush,' he replied. 'I've already told the station I'll be back in an hour.'

'Ah,' Pepe said, excited. 'Good news. Francesca lasagne ready ten minute–'

'Oh, no. I couldn't possibly impose. I just need to ask Gabriella a few questions, then I'm heading back to the station.'

'*Si, si.* Terrible tragedy for little Leigh,' Pepe said. A tear rolled down his cheek.

Gabriella walked in, right on cue. 'Okay, Lieutenant. I'm all yours.'

Within that split second of realising why he was sitting in her parents' home, she burst into tears. 'I'm sorry. I still can't get my head around what's happened. Every time we saw each other, we'd run in for a hug, which would carry on for far too long, while we gushed about our lives.' As she sat, she flourished a tissue to her raw, chapped nose and blew into its recesses. Her eyes were puffy and red. 'Anastasia and I honestly don't know how we're going to cope without her. How can we help you find this evil killer?'

Pepe stood beside her, his hand on her shoulder in support.

'Did Leigh have any enemies?' Craig asked. 'Maybe someone who wanted to harm her?'

'No, no. Absolutely not. Everyone loved Leigh.'

Craig lowered his voice. 'Has she had any altercations with anyone? Especially since her arrival in Champaign?'

'Not to my knowledge, but she did mention that cracks had developed in her relationship with Chad. She was furious with him for not spending much time with her in Australia. They'd apparently planned for him to go over on a regular basis, but he never did.' She shook her head. 'I remember her saying he always came up with ridiculous excuses for not being able to go. A few days ago, she told Anastasia and me that she'd had enough and was seriously considering breaking up with him. It wasn't much of a surprise to us – we knew what he was like. I think Leigh had come to the realisation that there was more to life than having a boyfriend who didn't treat her the way she had hoped for.' Rubbing her arms, Gabriella looked down.

Craig scratched his temple as he gave his next question some thought, then cocked his head to one side. 'So, did Leigh have anyone else on the radar?'

'Absolutely not! She was a one-man woman,' Gabriella replied rather indignantly, raising her eyebrows. 'So many men showed an interest in Leigh; she could've had anyone she wanted, but she wasn't interested. She was in a good place in her life, Lieutenant. Winning in Beijing inspired her to go for a back-to-back win in London. She was more focused than I'd ever seen her before.'

Craig studied her face, listening intently to her every word. She sighed. 'When the festivities of this trip were over, she was going to fly to Denmark to spend two weeks with her brother. She hadn't seen him in ages. Oh, my soul, she was so excited to see him... it would've been her first trip to Denmark. Gary had arranged an incredible itinerary for her. Then, it would've been back to the grindstone – straight back to Melbourne. She only envisioned another year in Australia, then would've returned stateside next fall for good.'

'Well, you've certainly been most helpful,' Craig said with a genuine smile, the lines around his eyes crinkling. He looked at his watch, a sleek silver band clasped around his wrist. 'I need to get back to the station, but if you remember anything else...'

He stared at Gabriella with a flicker of hope in his chest. Every bit of information he could get would be critical in catching Leigh's killer. Gabriella looked back at him with tears streaming down her face.

'I'll rack my brain for anything else that may assist in your investigation,' she said in a trembling voice. 'All I want is for this murderer to be caught before he can cause harm to someone else. Justice must prevail for my friend.'

As Gabriella stood up, the world around her spun as if she were on a tilt-a-whirl. Vertigo engulfed her, and she fell into her father's arms. Pepe gave her a comforting hug, just as any father who loved his daughter to distraction would do.

This emotional scene was thwarted by clinking silverware, clanging dishes and hurried footsteps in the next room as Francesca set the table for lunch. The welcoming aroma of cooked pasta filled the air.

'Gabriella, *cara mia*, please come help Mama,' Francesca bellowed from the dining room.

'Okay, Mama. I'll be right there.'

With a parting wave to Craig, she hurried to join her mother.

'*Cara*, you tell Lieutenant he stay for lunch, yes? He eat lasagne.'

'He needs to go back to the station, Mama. I'm sure he wasn't expecting to have lunch with us anyway.'

'No, no, no. He's a man, must eating. Look, time no, come bring for Lieutenant now.'

Gabriella turned in the direction of the living room and heard floorboards creaking towards the front door. Against her usual quiet nature, she let out a sharp shout that echoed throughout the passage. 'Lieutenant, please don't leave now. My mom insists that you stay for lunch, and she's serving as we speak!'

Taken aback, Craig sported the deer-in-the-headlights look. Pepe swiftly placed his hand under Craig's arm and escorted him down the hallway.

'Francesca, she's *fattore dominante*,' Pepe confided. The men shared a chuckle. Craig walked dutifully with Pepe and Gabriella into the dining room, to be met by this larger-than-life Italiano mama.

'*Ciao, buon pomeriggio,* Lieutenant, please sit,' Francesca said. An overwhelming greeting from a vibrant and attractive fifty-something lady. Craig instantly noted how well-dressed she was under her apron, and how her big brown eyes radiated warmth and sincerity.

She's so hospitable, just like my mom, he thought. *So regal. I reckon this dame could pass as an opera singer and pull off an epic vibrato!*

He gave her a large grin as he took his seat at the table laden with food. The bright red lipstick on her fairly narrow lips likely wasn't going to be there for much longer, with all the talking she'd been doing ever since he first walked into their home.

'All peoples love Francesca lasagne,' Pepe said, the pride in his eyes palpable. 'You eating salad, yes?'

'*Buon appetite*,' Francesca declared. The sun streamed in through the floor-to-ceiling windows and fell on her beaming face.

While eating, Gabriella suddenly put down her knife and fork. 'I've just remembered something.'

'Oh?' said Craig, enjoying his tasty mouthful.

'You know how I mentioned Leigh leaving Chad?'

'Yes?'

'Well… Leigh probably wouldn't have told him, as she was going to drop that bombshell on the day of her departure.'

'Hmm. Interesting. I'll make a note of that.' Craig took a small book out of his pocket and quickly scrawled down the words. Tomato sauce on the side of his thumb smeared the page.

'As I said before, Lieutenant, I'll try to remember all the conversations we had recently. Rest assured, if there is anything, I'll call you immediately.' Gabriella's frown disappeared, replaced by an infectious grin with sparkling white teeth.

'I'd certainly appreciate that, Gabriella. Thank you!' Craig flashed her a big smile. He picked up a napkin, dabbed at the page and removed the remaining traces of the delicious lasagne.

He was anxious to excuse himself. The hour had turned into two.

Shit, I need to think of the right words to leave. How can I do it without being rude?

As he pondered over a few scenarios, he listened to the memory of his late mother's voice, thin and warbling like a clogged whistle.

Craig, you do not leave the table before your plate is cold. That is appalling etiquette! Don't you dare embarrass me.

'Lieutenant Ryan,' Gabriella said. She'd sensed the dilemma in his eyes. 'Please don't feel obliged to stay. We know you're a busy man.'

'Well then, thank you. I'll take your advice. I honestly don't mean to be rude, but there are matters requiring my immediate attention, and time is of the essence. Mr and Mrs Cantrello, I would like to thank you most kindly for your wonderful hospitality and very delicious meal. Mrs Cantrello, you make one hell of a mean lasagne.'

'You come anytime, Lieutenant. Francesca happy you happy, yes?' she said, with a broad smile.

+ + +

As Craig pulled up at the precinct, Cody ran towards him. *What the hell has happened now?* Craig thought, with an internal groan.

'Lieutenant!' Cody shouted. 'I'm so relieved you're finally here. This envelope has me freaked out.'

'Give me time to park,' Craig yelled back, and took the last puff of his cigarette. 'I'm sure another five minutes isn't going to make any difference.'

Cody retreated and blew out an exaggerated sigh. When Craig got out of the car, he immediately observed Cody's police-issued gun. It was dull and sat unusually low in its holster.

'When did you last clean your Glock?' he asked, stepping up his pace to the building.

'Um, a few weeks ago, Lieutenant,' Cody replied. He gave it a quick wipe on his shirt and held his breath in case Craig turned around.

'You're bloody lucky I have bigger fish to fry, Waterman,' Craig snapped back as he entered the building. 'Make sure it's sparkling in the morning.'

He headed straight to his office. On his desk lay a weird, grubby envelope.

'Cody,' he shouted through the closed door. 'Who else has handled this envelope?'

Cody sprinted into his office. 'Only me, Lieut,' he said, breathless.

'Did you put on your latex gloves before you picked it up?'

'Of course. Isn't that the first thing we get taught at the Academy?'

'Don't get clever with me, boy. You can go back to what you were doing. Close the door behind you.'

While Craig put on his gloves, he remembered Cody's comment about the sender's address. He turned over the envelope. Only his name and the physical address of the precinct were featured. No number, no zip code, and no official post office stamp. Unease slithered down his spine.

This bloody thing was hand-delivered.

The paper felt thick. As he opened the envelope, an 'L' cut out from a newspaper dropped onto his desk. Startled, he pulled the note out and read its contents.

The letters were cut out from a newspaper and neatly put together, spelling out the words. The fallen 'L' was from the word 'fell'.

How ironic, Craig thought. He turned the note over to see if there was anything else. There wasn't.

His eyelids clamped together as he mumbled, 'What the fuck is going on here?' He began to circle his office. 'This is the work of a deranged psycho. Obviously above average intelligence and a master of mind games.' He slammed his hands down on the desk, before composing himself and sitting down.

'Cody! Get in here, now!' he yelled, securing his face into his hands, elbows steady on the desk.

Cody hurried back in. His throat was dry. His palms moistened. Without giving it a thought, he wiped his hands on his pants.

'You wanted me, Lieut?' he asked, clicking his shoes together.

'Get this down to Fingerprints. Tell them to put a rush on it. I need to know if this cunning little prick left anything on this pathetic piece of paper.'

As Cody fumbled on his gloves, Craig tried to disassociate himself from the situation. His cell phone rang just as Cody scurried out with the letter. It was Gabriella.

'Lieutenant,' she said. 'I thought I'd give you a heads up: Anastasia is flying back to London on Friday. She mentioned she hasn't heard from you yet, so I thought you may want to get into contact with her.'

'Thank you, Gabriella. I'll call her right away.'

+   +   +

Meanwhile, the man was pacing around in his basement. Surely, Craig would've received his letter by now, so what to do next?

'I think I'll let him stew for a couple of days. What do you think, Surly?' he muttered, then paused. 'Quite right you are, Rip. We don't want to give him too much to work on now, do we?'

He stretched luxuriously. 'I'm absolutely loving all this attention, Surly. Never in a million years did I believe I'd be such a celebrity. Headlines in the newspaper, nightly reports on TV, all those people talking about me... my sack, this is exhilarating! Now, time to get started on the next cryptic clue.'

The already rampant pounding of his heart accelerated. 'Oh, this is extraordinary,' he bellowed, his cheeks lifting as his lips parted way for an uncontrollable laugh.

Chapter 11

When Craig arrived at Anastasia's parents' Tuscan-styled home on Wednesday afternoon, he couldn't help but notice all the cars parked outside, cluttering the leafy street. It looked like Grand Central Station's car park.

Shit, I hope I'm not crashing a party, he thought. *There'll be zero chance of Anastasia's undivided attention. For fuck's sake, I need to speak to her before she leaves!*

He thrust his weight behind his finger as he pressed the doorbell. The Carlyles weren't in the same social circle as the O'Riellys and Cantrellos; however, they all treated each other with mutual respect and, over the years, had gotten to know each other well. They had one important thing in common: love for their daughters.

Anastasia opened the door. Her eyes twinkled, lighting up the dimples embedded in her cheeks.

'Good day, Lieutenant Ryan. I do apologise for the full house. I've just received the most amazing news. My agent flew in this morning to tell me that my European tour has been modified to a world tour!'

'That's fantastic. Congratulations!'

Her smile faded, as tears pooled in her quivering eyes. 'But in the same breath, Lieutenant, my guilt envelops me. I feel pressure building in my lower abdomen for being this happy in view of everything that happened to Leigh. I try — albeit not so successfully — to remember she was one of my ardent supporters and would've been at all my concerts, front row seat.' A solitary tear rolled down her cheek. 'My apologies. I've been rambling on, and we haven't progressed any further than the entrance hall.'

She leaned forward, hand to his ear. 'Please follow me. I'll lead the way to my dad's study, where we can talk in some peace and quiet.'

They walked down the long stretch of hallway, footsteps echoing on the hardwood floors. Craig could hear the drone of voices from another room. Anastasia swiftly closed the study door behind them, and the voices faded into oblivion.

'May I offer you a coffee?' she asked. 'Or a beer?'

'I'm still on official business, so coffee would be great. Thanks.' Craig settled into the comfort of the plush La-Z-Boy chair opposite her father's old-fashioned mahogany desk.

'I'll be right back.' Anastasia clicked her fingers and bounced towards the door. Minutes later, the aroma of two freshly brewed long blacks filled the air as she returned.

'Cheers,' she said. They clinked their mugs. 'Lieutenant, how is your investigation going? Are you any closer to finding Leigh's killer?'

'We're still working around the clock. So, tell me, are you aware of any altercations Leigh may have been in recently?'

'Nothing springs to mind, apart from the fact that Leigh was going to break up with Chad. That was going to happen the morning of her departure; that way, there'd be no time for Chad to try and talk her out of it. She was so ready to release herself from his manipulative grip.'

Sighing, she took a seat behind her father's desk. 'I know they hadn't spent much time together. Chad went away on business recently – to San Francisco if I'm not mistaken. Leigh was furious with him for scheduling his trip then, knowing full well that she'd be in Champaign. When she confronted him about it, he brushed it off and said she was being ridiculous.'

Anastasia pursed her lips, staring at the picture hanging on one wall – the same graduation photo Craig had seen on the Cantrellos' mantelpiece. 'She was bitterly upset with his reaction. It was the final straw that broke the camel's back, as she told Gabriella and me. She kept repeating herself, tsk-tsking through a crooked mouth, and bit her nails to the quick. She was done with such an uncaring, self-absorbed man. I think she used the word "narcissist" multiple times. And that's when she declared with no uncertainty that she was leaving him. We both reassured her that she could do much better than an asshole like Chad.'

She shook her head. 'To be perfectly honest, Lieutenant, I think Chad was intimidated by her fame and did everything in his power to swing the limelight onto himself instead. He's a master of deception. Believe me, when needed, he can turn on that charm second to none. Do you know what I mean?'

'I'm starting to get the picture. Did he ever display any form of violence towards Leigh?' Craig asked, biting the inside of his cheek.

Distinct vertical lines appeared between Anastasia's brows. 'Not to my knowledge. As far as I'm aware, their altercations were purely verbal; in saying that I'll never forget how he thrived on emotionally blackmailing poor Leigh. What that man put her through...' She hung her head, her shoulders slumping. Her chin trembled. 'I'm a terrible friend.'

'Hey,' Craig said, blinking rapidly and rubbing at his own jaw. 'It'll be okay. He'll get what he deserves.'

She paused for a moment and regained her composure. 'Everyone knows Chad loves the girls. We always suspected he had a thing for someone at his office.' She rolled her eyes. 'Chad thinks he's quite a stud, but physically violent. I don't think so. Then again, who knows what really happens behind closed doors?'

'What–'

'Wait a moment,' she said. 'I recall Leigh had coffee with Marco Carrera a couple of times.'

'Your old teacher?'

'Oh, yes. We all love him to bits. He's so easy to talk to and is always willing to lend an ear. Maybe she might've said something to him?'

Glancing at the photo on the wall, Craig knew Marco would be the next person he needed to speak to.

'Anastasia, you've been such a great help. Thank you for your time. So, when does your tour start?'

'We're still planning. In three months, maybe?'

'Well, good luck. Not that you need it, of course; I'm sure you'll be a huge hit. You certainly have plenty of fans out there.'

'You're too kind! Before I go on tour, though, I'll be in LA with Gabriella for the Academy Awards ceremony. I'm convinced she's going to win an Oscar. The little star has already bagged a Golden Globe, so wouldn't that be amazing?'

Again, she broke down suddenly in a flood of tears. 'I'm so sorry, Lieutenant,' she said in a soft voice. 'The cold hard fact of it all is that the third of the three musketeers isn't with us anymore. We always believed we'd grow old together and end up in a retirement centre overlooking the Pacific Ocean, where we'd reminisce for hours about the wonderful lives we'd been blessed with.'

While she wiped her eyes, Craig stood and put a hand on her shoulder. 'Whoever's responsible will pay,' he said. 'And Leigh would be so proud of you, Anastasia. You keep doing the best you can for her, yeah?' She nodded. 'I promise you, this will all be over soon.'

As Craig got back into his car, his cell phone rang. Looking at the ID, he saw it was the fingerprint department. He answered without a greeting. 'Did you find anything?'

'No, Lieutenant.' The caller inhaled deeply. 'We doubled up on everything, still came up with nothing. This guy sure knows what he's doing.'

'Not the answer I needed right now, but thanks for the call. See you in the morning,' Craig muttered. He drove off, feeling very despondent.

It's time to get back to basics, he thought.

Chapter 12

The next morning, Craig laboured up the worn steps leading to the crime laboratory, his feet shuffling against the rough surface. Cursing his beloved cigarettes, he at last reached the second-floor landing. Hushed whispers and clinking equipment filled his ears. He took a deep breath and pushed open the heavy metal door.

Inside, the walls were speckled by years of wear and tear. Fluorescent lights flickered overhead, casting a pale glow over the scene. Craig knew this place like the back of his hand – the forensic evidence technicians, scenes-of-crime officers, laboratory analysts, and forensic scientists were his allies in solving cases. He greeted each familiar face with a nod, weaving his way through the maze of desks and equipment. His eyes were drawn to the rows of test tubes and microscopes, each one a critical tool in piecing together the puzzle of a crime scene.

Finally, he arrived at his destination – the evidence room. As he entered, heart racing, hoping for good news, he could smell the faint aroma of chemicals and see the gleam of metal on shelves stacked high with boxes and envelopes. Craig knew that every piece of evidence in this room held a clue that could crack open the toughest case.

'Craig, over here,' came a deep female voice from behind a computer screen. All he could see was a bejewelled hand with bright red nails waving energetically at him. 'I've got somethin' you may find interestin'.'

I wish all the lab analysts were as efficient as this beaut, Craig thought, as he rounded Coco's desk. She could be Whoopi Goldberg's twin for sure!

'This is the most recent finding,' she said, twirling her dreads. 'Evidence collected from the duct tape found at the scene of the crime includes multiple hairs from an unknown long-haired dog breed and fibres from what could be a purple rug. How many of your suspects have a dog, and how many have a purple rug?'

'What about the button? Anything on that?'

'Ya think I'm Speedy Gonzales or somethin'? I'm still workin' on that. One thing at a time. Don't worry, Lieut – we'll get this psycho.'

'I'm counting on you, Whoopi,' he said with a huge grin. They high fived with such vigour it sent her dreadlocks in all directions.

He slipped back into his car, and the familiar tune of Kirsten's favourite song filled the air. As the melody washed over him, his thoughts wandered to the case at hand. He'd need to check in with Kirsten soon and see if she had any new leads.

Gripping the steering wheel tightly, he headed towards the scene of the crime, a knot of anxiety growing in his stomach. When he pulled up to it, his heart sank. The forensic tent had been dismantled, and the yellow police tape had been removed. It was just an empty plot of land once again, but it had an eerie feel to it. The kind that left chills down his spine.

He scoured the area, walking the perimeter of where Leigh's lifeless body had been found five days before. He paced back and forth, desperately searching for anything that might lead him to a break in the case. The only solace he found was in the sound of rustling leaves and the soft crunch of gravel beneath his feet. The evidence they'd collected thus far had yielded few results. Coco's comment about the suspects owning a dog or purple rug was a long shot, but it was something. Something to hold onto, something to give him hope.

And in this line of work, he thought, *sometimes that's all you have.*

Craig walked briskly back to his car, his mind racing with questions. He needed to speak to their former teacher. Surely, Carrera could provide some insight into what had happened.

Craig looked at his watch and calculated that the school would be taking a recess soon. He decided to take his chances and headed towards Brentwood Park High.

As he waited in the foyer, as instructed by the secretary, Craig gazed at the pictures of the school's alumni adorning the walls. He was lost in thought when he suddenly felt a tap on his shoulder. He turned around to see a man with striking green eyes.

'Lieutenant Ryan, I presume?' The words were clear, almost musical, with a hint of a Spanish accent.

Craig took a deep breath. 'Your reputation precedes you, Mr Carrera. My daughter and her friends always speak so highly of you.' He extended his hand.

With a demure smile, Carrera accepted it. 'The principal has offered us his office for privacy. Please follow me.'

Craig felt quite at ease with this charismatic man. Carrera had a calming aura about him and was immaculate from his grooming to his attire.

'Lieutenant…' he started, his voice cracking. He cleared his throat, before trying again. 'I'm absolutely devastated. We're still in shock, I think. No one believed that something like this could happen.' He grimaced. 'I was so excited to see the girls again. We all were. To have the school's most famous alumni as the guests of honour at our one hundredth anniversary… this was truly a celebration with a difference. This city has never experienced anything of this magnitude before. We've been planning this for months.' Tears welled in his eyes.

'I'm fully aware of that, Mr Carrera—'

He shook his head. 'Marco, please.'

'Alright, Marco. Do you know of anyone who'd want to harm Leigh?'

'No, Lieutenant. Leigh had absolutely no enemies. She was loved by everyone; to refer to her as Champaign's sweetheart is quite the understatement. She has – I'm sorry.' He swallowed deeply. 'She *had* the most beautiful disposition. She was so kind and caring. Always more concerned about others' wellbeing than her own. She was just a lovely person, inside and out.'

He wiped his eyes. 'I can't for the life of me fathom why anyone would do something so hideous to such a gorgeous young woman. Do you have any suspects, Lieutenant?'

'I'm not at liberty to disclose that information. Let's just say we're working on it.' Craig watched him closely. 'The girls trusted you. Confided in you. What do you know about her relationship with Chad, her boyfriend?'

'Well, I believe they had their ups and downs, like any other couple. Nothing serious enough to be concerned about. They always seemed to work out their problems, however big or small. I do know she was very excited to be reunited with Chad again, after her long stint away from home. She mentioned he was putting pressure on her to give up swimming. What?'

'I know – outrageous. Her goal was to get back-to-back medals. Nothing was going to stand in her way.'

'And that's it? Nothing else?'

Marco hesitated. 'Lieutenant, I want to help you. I honestly do,' he said. 'There was something else… but if it gets out, it could mean Leigh's name being dragged through the mud, and I could never do that to her. You know what Champaign is like if it gets a hint of scandal.'

'What is it?' Craig pushed. 'Marco, please. If you know something, you have to tell me.'

He shook his head. 'No. I shouldn't have spoken. I'm sorry.'

'You want to help me find Leigh's killer, yes?'

'Of course I do. More than anything.' He hung his head, dejected. 'If I tell you, Lieutenant, it must stay between us. No one else can know – not even your team.

All Leigh has left is her legacy. The least I can do is protect that with my life.'

'Sure. Just between us.' Craig shifted closer.

Marco took a deep breath. 'Leigh and I… we were together. We reconnected in her time back in Champaign, and… well, I'll spare you the details, Lieutenant, but if Chad found out about us? That boy had a temper, even back in his school days. He was a nightmare to teach.' He choked up. 'If he hurt her because of me…'

Craig offered Marco a tissue. 'Do you think Chad knew?'

'I don't know. I don't think Leigh would've told him – I don't think she told anyone – but it's all I can think of. Who else would want to hurt such a kind soul?'

Marco stared into empty space, taking a moment to recompose himself, before he noticed the clock on the wall. 'Oh. I'm sorry, Lieutenant, but I'd better get back to class. You know what these kids are like when their teacher isn't in the room!' He excused himself and left Craig to see himself out of the school building.

Craig always seemed to think more rationally with a cigarette in his hand. As he lit up and exhaled on the way to the parking lot, thoughts of Kirsten came streaming through his mind.

I need to call her now.

Chapter 13

'Good day to you, my lovely lady. How art thou?'

Kirsten's heart skipped a beat as she heard Craig's smooth words crackle through the phone. 'All the better for hearing your voice,' she replied, a slight smile playing on her lips.

Craig wasted no time. 'Kirsten, can you meet me at the station, in, say, twenty minutes?'

'Of course. I'll see you there,' she said, quickly reaching for her lipstick to touch it up.

As he ended the call, Craig couldn't help but picture Kirsten in his mind. Her beautiful big brown eyes and elegant figure always left him breathless. He thought a different hairdo from her stylish bob would enhance her beauty, but he knew better than to suggest anything that might upset her.

Driving her convertible down the busy streets, Kirsten let the wind play with her hair. Her scarf almost slipped away as she sang along with her favourite tune. She too was a smoker and never left home without her diamond-encrusted cigarette holder tucked away in her purse, along with the matching case and lighter.

The pair pulled up to the station in perfect unison, grinning at each other in mutual admiration. Before heading into Craig's office, they decided to indulge in a quick smoke break, exchanging easy jokes and pleasantries.

'These bloody new rules are insane,' Craig said.

Kirsten raised her eyebrows as she exhaled. 'Surely there must be more important issues to address in this world than where we can smoke,' she declared, and took another puff of her cigarette.

A few minutes later, Craig closed the door while Kirsten wiped dust off a chair and sat down. 'I see you're still so damned pedantic,' he said with a chuckle, settling into his own very uncomfortable chair.

'You know I don't do dirt. So, tell me, when did this office last get a clean?' She continued to wipe everything around her, oblivious to the look on Craig's face. 'Oh, my soul, I wouldn't cope here. Not for a day.'

She fixed her scarf, crossed her legs elegantly and took a small leopard-print mirror out of her purse, ensuring she didn't have a hair out of place.

Craig smiled. 'Right, then. Let's get down to business. What have you heard out there?'

'Unfortunately, nothing you don't already know,' she said, shrugging. 'Everything seems to have gone quiet. Like the calm before the storm.'

'I wouldn't quite put it like that, dear heart.' He sighed, an almost resigned look on his face. 'Well, I've just had a chat to Leigh's former teacher, Marco Carrera – he certainly lives up to the hype. He mentioned Chad was angling at Leigh giving up swimming. Know anything about that?'

'Absolutely not! Leigh had reached her pinnacle in swimming, that thought would never have even crossed her mind. Where'd he hear that garbage?'

'He said Leigh told him on one of their coffee dates.'

'What else did she reportedly have to say at those coffee dates?' she asked, the corners of her mouth curling up.

'Don't bloody well interrogate me, Kirsten,' Craig snapped. 'I thought we were going to have our usual brainstorming session.'

'Oh, Craig!' She raised her hands in mock surrender. 'I do apologise. There's just so much of this he-said, she-said nonsense going on. I can't help but feel we're getting nowhere fast. Most of what I hear these days I take with a pinch of salt.'

Kirsten paused, biting her lip. 'I must say… something about that teacher doesn't quite sit right with me. Can't put my finger on it, but it niggles me just the same. He's charming. Seductive. Maybe enough to get a girl to let her guard down.'

Craig pondered her words, thinking back to the desperation in Marco's eyes, what he'd revealed, and the promise Craig had made him. Craig was usually quite good at reading people – perk of the job – and from what he could tell, Marco Carrera seemed solid. Generally remorseful and torn up about Leigh's death. It didn't fit with the killer's profile at all.

'I've thought about it, sure,' he said. 'Everyone's a suspect to me, regardless of circumstance, until proven otherwise. Yes, his charisma works to his advantage, and he has swept a lot of people away. Looks can be deceiving.' He rubbed his chin. 'Still, he seems genuine. The girls adore him, and that ridiculous sloppy handshake of his is testament to his soft – or maybe weak – character.'

'Yeah,' she said, pursing her lips. 'Maybe I'm wrong. It's just... he's so sickly sweet, and he never has a hair out of place. He's almost too perfect to be real!'

'Now there's the Kirsten I adore,' he teased. 'If someone doesn't show her in the first moment of meeting that they have more than enough oomph, she thinks they've got something to hide.'

'Most people do,' she said.

'And some are just nice.'

She released a small chuckle. 'You're right. I must learn to give people the benefit of the doubt, I guess.'

Craig's mind turned back to the case at hand. From what Marco had said, Chad was looking even more plausible, but he couldn't exactly divulge what he knew, not even to Kirsten. He was a man of his word.

He turned back to the scrawled notes on the whiteboard. 'I'm still leaning towards Chad,' he said. 'He had the motive and most certainly the means, but part of me says he's not a killer. He's the type that would get someone else to do his dirty work for him, which brings me back to those girls at his office. Feisty little bitches, the two of them: very capable of hatching a plan and bringing it to fruition. And they're certainly not the brightest. If Chad had asked them to get rid of Leigh, they might have. Only problem is, they're too small; that walk down to the ravine is at one helluva gradient. I can't see those high-heeled divas carrying a body down there.'

He let his head fall onto the hard wooden desk. 'And now we're back to square one. Again.'

There was a knock at the door. Craig grunted.

'You can come in,' Kirsten said.

Cody walked in with a perplexed look on his face. 'This just arrived. It's addressed to you, Lieutenant.'

It was a cardboard box with the zip code 46201 clearly stamped on the front, instead of the Champaign code he'd been expecting.

'Where's it from, Cody?' Craig asked.

'Indianapolis.'

'So,' Craig said. 'This little asshole wants to play games.' He turned to Kirsten. 'Bet you a million bucks this isn't from an Indianapolis resident – takes, what, two hours to drive there? How stupid does he think we are?'

Putting on his latex gloves, he carefully opened the parcel, Kirsten and Cody waiting with bated breath to see what was inside.

'What's this?' he said, screwing up his face. He picked up an envelope, peering into the box just in case there was something else inside. There wasn't. He carefully opened the envelope to reveal another letter made with newspaper cuttings.

'Fucking hell! This psycho is becoming too brazen.' Craig banged his fist on his desk, glancing at his car keys. 'Kirsten, you up for a ride to Indianapolis? Let's hit Interstate 74 now, and I'll buy you lunch in Danville. Deal?'

'Why the hell not? I'll contact my assistant and ask her to take over for me today. Finding Leigh's killer is paramount right now. Let's hit the road, Jack. I'm quickly nipping down to the bathroom; I'll meet you at the car in two.'

As she scurried off, Craig took another look at the parcel and noticed it had been mailed two days ago.

A fresh trail. Craig grinned. *I'm onto you now, bastard.*

Chapter 14

Craig and Kirsten decided to drive straight to Indianapolis and stop in Danville on the way back, as every second counted against them when they were off the killer's trail. They made the trip in record time, pulling up at the downtown post office way under the two hours Craig had predicted.

'Why do all these buildings look and feel the same inside?' Kirsten whispered, as she nudged Craig.

'Bureaucracy,' he whispered back, shrugging. He was more concerned about why they were there in the first place.

They were ushered into the manager's office by a middle-aged woman. Kirsten immediately began sizing her up. She'd obviously been working there her entire adult life, and if she had to smile, her face would likely crack. Her outfit was as drab as the interior of the building.

God, I wouldn't be seen dead in that, Kirsten thought.

'Please take a seat,' the drab mouth said, in a stern English accent that didn't quite match her demeanour and calculatedly unattractive appearance. 'Mr Baldwin shall be with you shortly.'

Craig scanned the office for any sign of CCTV cameras, feeling a wave of unease wash over him. His eyes landed on an ancient, strange-looking contraption perched high up in the corner of the ceiling. His mind raced to piece together a plan of action.

The sound of footsteps outside caught his attention. Kirsten was alert too, turning to face the door just as it swung open. In walked Mr Baldwin, his eyes darting between the two of them. Craig and Kirsten rose to their feet, hands extended in greeting. After a brief exchange of introductions, Mr Baldwin gave a wry grin.

'What brings a lieutenant from Champaign all the way to my humble abode?' he asked.

Craig wasted no time in launching into the reason for their visit. 'Sir, we need to access any CCTV footage you might have in and around this building.'

Mr Baldwin's face darkened. 'We do have cameras, but they're outdated, practically prehistoric. I've been requesting upgrades for ages, but no one seems to care.' He shook his head. 'Still, we'll help you in any way we can. The footage we have covers two weeks. What's your timeframe?'

'We think the suspect might've been here two days ago.'

As Craig spoke, Kirsten passed the box to Mr Baldwin, who studied it intently. Suddenly, his face lit up. 'The ink on this box is much darker than usual,' he said. 'I'll call Ms Appleton into my office right away.'

With that, he picked up the phone. Craig felt a sense of cautious optimism growing within him. Perhaps this old piece of equipment would be their key to unlocking the mystery of the dreaded letters.

'Do you require something, sir?' Ms Appleton enquired, marching into the office.

'Yes, Myrtle. When did we last change the ink refill of the main stamp for parcels?'

'It was done... Tuesday morning, directly after the tea break.' She pushed her glasses closer to the bridge of her nose. 'I recall this fact as it was I who issued the directive for this to be done. Is there a problem?'

'No, no. Merely an enquiry. That is all, my dear. Thank you.' Mr Baldwin nodded his head, then tilted it slightly to dismiss her. She turned on her heel and left.

'An efficient administrator,' he said, looking at two amused faces in front of him.

'I could do with some of that precision in my precinct,' Craig said, as they stood. 'What time does tea break end?'

'At 10:15.'

'Perfect. Let's start by looking at the tapes from then.'

The footage showed that the post office had been buzzing with activity on that Tuesday morning. People hurried in and out of the building, all with their own agendas. The task at hand was clear, and everyone was focused on it. It was almost as if they were racing against time.

At 10:45, a peculiar character caught Craig's attention. It was a man, but his appearance was unusual. He wore a hat and tortoiseshell-rimmed glasses with a red scarf around his neck. The heavy trench coat he'd bundled himself in partially covered the box under his arm, although as Mr Baldwin zoomed in on it, it did compare favourably to the one currently on the desk.

The outside camera footage revealed the mystery man's casual demeanour as he exited the post office and made his way down the street. He walked alone, and there was no sign of transportation nearby. He vanished without a trace.

'Shit,' Craig said. 'That's a bummer.'

'Well, it's something,' Kirsten said, squeezing his shoulder. 'It's more than what we had. And you never know, the footage could still prove quite useful.' She turned to Mr Baldwin. 'Will we be able to make a copy of the tape as evidence?'

'Of course you may,' he said. 'It is my absolute pleasure to assist the Champaign police and perform my duty as required.'

A true civil servant, Craig thought.

As they raced back down Interstate 74, Craig gripped the steering wheel tight, breathing in the smoke trailing from Kirsten's cigarette. 'We need to touch base with Shelagh and Dylan. See how they're doing and find out about the men in Leigh's life.'

'Don't stress so much, Craig,' Kirsten said soothingly, and took a deep drag. 'You'll get your beast. All the pieces of the puzzle will fall into place, just like they always do.'

'I know that. It's just... this case is so close to home.' Craig slammed his fist down on the steering wheel. 'I want that bastard behind bars ASAP, with no chance of parole.'

Chapter 15

The leaves of the Autumn Blaze maple trees danced and twirled in the light breeze, painting the street they lined in vibrant hues of crimson. The sun was beginning to set, casting an orange glow across the sky. Today, however, Craig and Kirsten ignored this picture-perfect setting. There was another focus, and that was the O'Riellys' wellbeing.

Craig pulled up on the perfectly maintained circular drive outside the grand home. The sound of the tyres crunching on the paving echoed through the silence. For a while, neither of them made a move to exit the car.

'I wish we were here for a different reason. It never gets any easier,' Craig said, his voice heavy. Kirsten placed a gentle hand on his back, a small comfort amidst the turmoil.

As they made their way towards the entrance, the massive oak door towered over them. Dylan greeted them with a half-hearted smile, a shadow of his usual jovial self. Shelagh appeared moments later, her once bright and cheerful personality now diminished. Dylan led Craig towards the pub area, where the O'Riellys had installed a fully stocked bar, while the two women headed to the kitchen.

'How are you holding up?' Kirsten asked, enveloping Shelagh in a tender embrace.

Tears streamed down Shelagh's face. 'I'm not coping at all. My heart has been shattered into a million pieces! Kirst, I can't live without my daughter. My head is fuzzy... this medication helps, but nothing eases the pain in my heart.'

Kirsten stood by her friend's side, offering tissues and a shoulder to cry on. Eventually, Shelagh's hysterical sobs subsided, and she took deep breaths to compose herself. 'I'm sorry,' she said.

'Don't you apologise. You cry as much as you need to. I'm here for you – that's what friends are for.'

'Would you like a coffee, Kirst? Or maybe something a tad stronger?' Shelagh asked, a small smile playing at the corners of her lips.

'I think a chilled glass of vino would go down well, honey,' Kirsten replied with a grateful grin.

They walked arm in arm to the pub, where the two men were engrossed in conversation. 'Are we interrupting something?' Kirsten asked.

'Not at all, ladies,' was Craig's hasty reply. 'I'm just bringing Dylan up to speed on the investigation.'

'What did you find? Did you get that evil monster, Craig?' Shelagh's lip curled with disdain.

'Unfortunately, not yet,' he said. 'We know the perpetrator is still at large in the Champaign area. At this stage, I'm not able to release any other information. But' – Craig pointed his finger upwards – 'you'll be the first to know the moment we nail this bastard. That's a promise I intend to keep.'

Shelagh twisted her hands together. 'This morning was the first time I'd had the courage to enter Leigh's room. I stood in the doorway for a while... there wasn't a thing out of place, the duvet on the bed still perfectly straight, with no creases. It was immaculate, just like my baby doll. Then it hit me like a ton of bricks that she was never coming back...'

She trailed off in sobs. Dylan carefully took her hand and gave it a squeeze, his own eyes welling up. Heavy silence surrounded the bar counter.

'I collapsed,' Shelagh finally said. 'Fell to the floor. I don't know for how long. For some reason, while I was lying there, I thought about her cell phone. She was so preoccupied, and always left it lying around somewhere. I guess a part of me was hoping to see it next to her bed, giving me a false glimmer of hope that she would return to get it, even though I know that could never happen.'

She lost her breath. This time, Dylan got off his bar stool and lovingly embraced her.

'So was her cell in her room?' Craig asked.

'That's what I'm trying to tell you! I searched again and again, looked in all her handbags, but came up with nothing. Now that I think about it... Craig, her new red Jimmy Choo bag is also missing. Did your officers take them in as evidence?'

Craig didn't recall seeing or hearing about a bag or phone; they would've been the first things he'd checked if they were with the body. Still, he might've missed something. Maybe Coco was still searching the items? No point in worrying the already-distraught parents.

'I'll check with forensics tomorrow morning,' he said. 'They have everything bagged and recorded, ready to be used as evidence to nail the bastard when this case goes to trial.'

+ + +

'My, my, what do we have here?' hissed the man, as he read the headline on the front page of the *Chronicle*.

NEW EVIDENCE COMES TO LIGHT ON LEIGH O'RIELLY'S MURDER

'What new evidence could this possibly be? I thought I had everything under wraps... surely, they're playing me. So, you *do* like to play games, Lieutenant! I knew it!'

He jumped in the air, then paused, running a hand through his hair.

'Whatever. Typical investigative scaring tactic. It ain't gonna work, you dickheads. That's just an insult to my intelligence.' He raised his eyebrows. 'I'm not falling into any of your traps. I'll keep going as I always do.'

A high-pitched, girlish giggle left him. 'So, Rip, did you manage to secure something from this little soiree?'

He rubbed his hands together. 'Of course, I did, Surl. You know I'm not an amateur. There's always got to be a little piece of the pie.'

Should I, shouldn't I, should I, shouldn't I? Nah, I'll wait another week or so before sending Craig another love letter. With all these little notes, he may even start falling for me!

He laughed at the prospect, breaking into a jig.

Yeah, just a little while longer...

+   +   +

As Craig drove towards the crime lab the following day, he couldn't shake off a feeling of unease. He hoped they had found the handbag and cell; he needed something positive now.

Looking up at the colonial building, he noticed it needed some TLC. Still, despite its faded paint and chipped walls, there was something grand about its stately windows and imposing architecture. Craig stubbed out his cigarette, feeling a sudden sense of appreciation for the building that housed some of the most important investigations in the city.

Inside, he was greeted by the familiar scent of antiseptic and sound of lab equipment. He headed straight for the scenes of crime department, where Coco was engrossed in her work.

Craig couldn't help but grin as he walked towards her, throwing his arm around her shoulders. 'How's my favourite gal doing?' he exclaimed.

'Ah, a hug so early in the mornin',' Coco said, laughing. She punched him lightly on the arm. 'Just what I needed to start my day. So, what's goin' on, Lieut?'

'I need to go through the items found at Leigh O'Rielly's crime scene. Are they still here, or have they been sent to the DA's office?'

'Nah, they're still here. Not all the results have come back yet.'

'Cool,' Craig replied, relieved. 'Do you think we could have a quick look now?'

'Course. Follow me.' Coco extended her arm in a bow-like movement. She led him through the open-plan offices and down a flight of stairs, into a room lit by a dim fluorescent overhead light.

'There's Leigh's belongings and all the other evidence we've managed to get,' she said. 'Take ya time, big man; I ain't in no hurry.'

Craig sifted through all the articles, but Leigh's handbag and cell phone were nowhere to be found. 'Is this everything?'

'Yeah, this is all that was recovered. What ya lookin' for?'

'Her cell phone and handbag. Shit, if they're not here… there's only two places they could be: at the crime scene or in the hands of the killer. I'm gonna head back to the crime scene now.' Craig turned to open the door. Stopping his babble, and stopping in his tracks, he said, 'You're the best, Coco. Thank you.'

'So formal, Lieut. What happened to Whoopi?' she asked, a deep chuckle stemming from her belly.

'Gotta keep some things official sometimes,' he said, winking. 'This room requires formality!'

As they walked along the corridor, Coco asked, 'Still no leads on the owner of a long-haired pooch and purple rug?'

'So far, nothing. I'll keep you in the loop.'

He said his goodbyes and left. The moment he got back to his car, he radioed through to the station. 'Cody, get a team down to Leigh O'Rielly's crime scene immediately. I'm on my way there now. We've got some digging to do.'

As he sped towards the scene, Craig's mind raced. Time was running out; they needed to find some concrete evidence before it was too late. He directed his team to search every inch of the area once again. They worked tirelessly, scouring every tree, bush, and shrub for clues.

The day wore on, and Craig's heart sank. Despite their best efforts, they'd come up empty-handed once again. No designer handbag, no cell phone, and no new evidence.

Sitting on the ground, dejected and exhausted, he thought back to the AT&T records he'd received earlier. They showed that the last call on Leigh's phone had been made at 4.30 p.m. on the day she was murdered. It was a dead end.

'That's it, then,' Craig said, bending his head forward and sighing. 'That bastard has obviously got the phone and handbag, and he won't be getting rid of them any time soon.'

Deep in thought, he barely heard his phone ring. He picked it up on the last chime, trying to sound calm. 'Hello?'

'Hi there, Lieutenant. It's Gabriella. Just thought I'd check in with you for an update.'

'We're still working around the clock, don't you worry. When we get our breakthrough, you'll be notified. How's Oscar fever in LA treating you?'

'It's amazing! I've been completely overwhelmed by all the attention – they're making such a fuss over me. Just being considered in the same class as my fellow nominees, people I've looked up to for years, is humbling. My dream has most certainly come true.' Her voice trembled. 'I still can't believe Leigh's not here to share this with me. That's the worst part of it all.'

'Don't worry, my girl. We'll get this monster.'

'Oh, yes – before I forget, the other reason I called was to let you know that I had a Skype chat with Chad last night. Would you believe he was planning to propose to Leigh the night before she was due to leave?'

His heart skipped a beat. Surely, he'd misheard. 'What?'

'I know. I didn't believe him at first, but... he meant it. I can tell when people are putting on an act, Lieutenant. Perks of the job and all.'

'What else did he say?'

'Apparently, Leigh was oblivious to what I'm going to tell you. Chad admitted to all his womanising over the past couple of years, expressing his desire to settle down and start a family with her. He was aware of the challenges, with her not being in the States, but he was ready to commit. He regretted all his messing around; he was certain she was the one for him. I saw the look on his face as he was talking. Believe me, he was sincere. He's not the Chad I thought I knew. Leigh's murder has rocked him rigid.'

Craig scoffed. 'He didn't seem very sorry when I spoke to him.'

'Well, you know what he's like—'

'An asshole?'

'...I was going to say *abrasive*, but yes. And, well, you've never liked him. He was probably putting on his cocky facade so you wouldn't think he felt guilty and arrest him.'

'Interesting. Very interesting. Thank you for sharing this information with me. Now, try to put all this drama out of your head and enjoy the fuss! I'll get the killer, and you get that little gold statuette and bring it home to Champaign. We're rooting for you.'

When Craig hung up, his mind was ticking over at an alarming rate. *Let's hope Chad's not a contender for an Oscar as well,* he thought, *with his own winning performance.*

Chapter 16

The sun had just begun to rise, casting a soft golden glow across the trees, filling the air with the cheerful melody of birds chirping and fluttering from branch to branch. As Craig dragged his feet up to the imposing entrance of the police station on Thursday morning, he suddenly felt a sharp pain in his stomach. It was an all-too-familiar feeling — a gut instinct telling him that something was about to go down.

Despite his lack of enthusiasm, he forced himself to greet everyone he passed with a polite nod or a tired smile. He'd been unable to relax over the weekend, and the past few days had been filled by fruitless work.

Inside his office, Craig switched on his computer, ready to begin the long day ahead of him. But just as he was getting settled in, there was a knock at his door. He didn't bother to hide his annoyance when he called, 'Come on in.'

When Cody entered with a small package in hand, Craig knew it was going to be a long day. 'Another one?' he asked.

Cody nodded, looking just as tired as Craig felt. 'It arrived about ten minutes ago. This time, the psycho paid some college freshman a hundred bucks to bring it here. We've got the kid in questioning, but it doesn't look very promising; he says he never saw the guy's face. Apparently, he was approached online and told to pick up a small box at the Arboretum this morning with the letter and money inside.'

'And we believe him?'

Cody shrugged. 'Hey, it's not like we're dealing with a criminal mastermind here. The kid started crying practically the second we put him in lockup.'

Grabbing his neglected cup of coffee, Craig took a long sip to help fortify himself against the challenges ahead. 'Can we at least trace this guy online?'

Cody shook his head. 'Not likely. Our cyber team is still looking, but it seems like he's covered his tracks pretty well.'

'Jeezus, this swine is relentless. Let's see what diabolic message he's got for us this time.' Craig cussed under his breath, then opened the letter, which was true to form and folded in the same manner as the other two. Taking a deep breath, he read aloud:

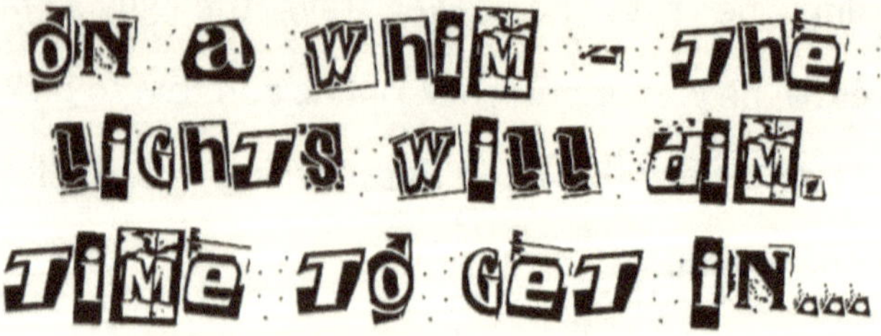

'*Time to get in*… What the fuck is this asshole playing at?' Craig bellowed, furiously kicking the side of his desk. 'Today we're gonna figure out these clues.'

Opening his drawers, he pulled out the other two notes, lining them up beside each other and inspecting them.

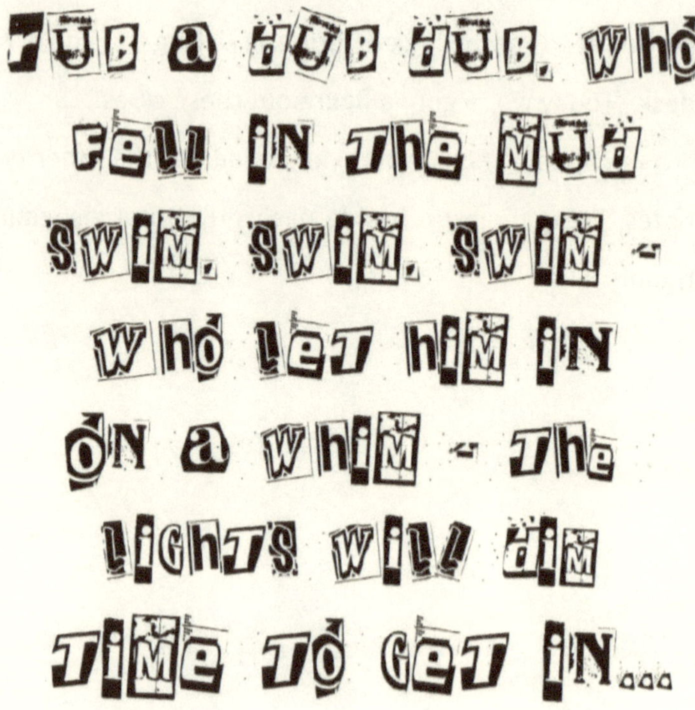

The penny suddenly dropped. 'Leigh knew her killer,' Craig said, his chest rising and falling vigorously. 'She knew the bastard!'

'You're sure?' Cody asked.

'It's right here!' Craig gestured to the papers. 'He ain't as clever as he thinks.' His stomach sank. 'I need to speak to Chad one more time.'

Minutes later, his phone rang, Coco's name flashing on the screen.

'Morning, Lieut,' she said. 'Sorry to be the bearer of bad news, but we got abso-bloody-lutely no luck with your results. Everything came back negative. This psycho is brilliant, man; he certainly knows what he's doing.'

'Ah, Whoops, it's the nature of the beast,' Craig said. 'We know we're not dealing with an amateur. We'll keep diggin'. He'll slip eventually, just like all the others before him. He's riding the crest of the wave right now – best he doesn't try surfing. The tide may just go out.'

+ + +

As Craig busied himself by running through every detail of the investigation, Chad too was sitting in his office, deep in thought. The guilt of his shenanigans with other women weighed heavily upon him. All he could think of was Leigh and the relationship they once had. His office door opened, and in sashayed Georgia.

'What do you want?' he snapped.

'You looked a little wound up when you walked in this morning. I thought I'd give you a nice, strong espresso, and maybe a neck massage to relieve you of all your tension. Who knows where that could lead?' She winked seductively, while sticking her index finger into her mouth.

'I'm not in the mood, Georgia – not now, not ever,' he said, an expressionless look on his face. 'The love of my life is dead. Whatever you think we may have had is over. I'm done with all this crap, so go and find someone else to play with. And while you're at it, pass the message on to Macy as well.'

For a moment, Georgia just stood there, totally taken aback. Taking a deep breath and swallowing hard, she turned on her stilettos and stormed out of his office.

'Georgia?' he called. She doubled back, hopeful.

'Yes, Chad?'

'You born in a stable? Close the door behind you.'

With a sharp-toothed grin, she slammed the door as hard as she could.

+ + +

At the same time, about an hour's drive from Champaign, Rip climbed out of his car. He stretched his legs, admiring the view from the top of the peak, overlooking the appealing countryside.

'This is going to be a crackerjack performance, if I say so myself,' he bellowed at the top of his voice, throwing his hands up in the air. As the dust stirred up, he coughed. 'Let's get down to some serious business!'

He opened the trunk of his car and pulled out something red. The sun caught upon the gold-plated fastener, the name *Jimmy Choo* shining brightly in that moment.

'Yes,' he said. 'I've got Jimmy, and what else could possibly be inside?'

He opened the bag and pulled out a cell phone. Holding it tightly, he raised it to the sky, squinting as he looked up. He dialled a number, let it ring three times, then cut the call and switched off the phone.

'Good luck tracing me here, Lieutenant!' He puffed out his chest and strutted back to the car. 'I'll be back in Champaign before you even know it.'

He drove off, music from his CD player thumping in his ears.

+ + +

As Chad reached his phone, he saw a missed call. His eyes widened.

'No. No, no. This must be a joke. What the fuck's going on?'

Head caught up in a whirling vortex of chaos, he fell back into his chair, pulling chunks out of his hair. Gradually, the spinning slowed. His mind started to clear, the world coming back into focus. He took a deep breath, picked up his keys, and rushed out of his office.

Lieutenant Ryan has got to see this.

Roz Potgieter

Chapter 17

'Hang upon someone's words.' A deep, theatrical voice filled the room as Rip relished the mellifluous sound of triumph that rang through his head. 'What springs to mind? Is it the cat that swallowed the cream? Perhaps. Nevertheless, let's persist in engaging in the activity... Come into my parlour, said the spider to the fly.'

As Champaign gradually recovered from the utter shock of Leigh's death a month before, the populace directed their attention to a new focal point beyond his web. Gabriella Cantrello had arrived back in the city, clutching an Oscar trophy in her hand. She was the first actress of this magnitude to hail from Champaign, and her face adorned every billboard and magazine cover in the area. She frequently graced the headlines of the *Chronicle* and was a constant fixture on the local TV channels.

While she appreciated the adulation, Gabriella felt more at ease with the unhurried pace of life back home. After the hustle and bustle of Los Angeles, it was a welcome respite to be back in familiar surroundings, far from the blinding glamour of Tinseltown's elite.

A week after her arrival, the Governor of Illinois extended an invitation for her to be the distinguished guest of his annual gala, a charity event to attract innovation-driven entrepreneurs to the state. It was one of the most anticipated events of the year, and anyone who was anyone would be in attendance. Who better than the highly decorated actress and golden child of Champaign to be the guest speaker?

'I'm actually kind of nervous, Mama,' Gabriella said to Francesca, passing the official invitation to her mother to read.

'Ah *mia bella*, you famous now,' Francesca said, stroking her daughter's beautiful locks. 'Everybody want *mia bambina* for every special function, *si!*'

'I guess, but I'm still not au fait with public speaking,' she said with a smile, not wanting to downplay her position on the pedestal her mother had so gallantly placed her on. 'Remember, this is real life. I'm not following a script.'

Gabriella had to remind herself that it wouldn't be like a scene from a movie... but public addresses never seemed to get any easier. Her Academy Awards speech had been an absolute nightmare! And her fiancé, Swedish mogul Bjorn Ericsson, was abroad growing his empire. Whom could she take as his substitute? Only one person's name surfaced in her mind.

'You know what, Mama? I think I should ask Marco Carrera to escort me to the ball. I'd feel uneasy going on my own, with Bjorn in South America.'

'I'm still wander with this man, why he no Italiano?' Francesca asked, looking bamboozled. She was like a stuck gramophone record about Marco having an Italian name; Gabriella had heard this statement a hundred times before.

'I'll call him right now.' Gabriella turned on her heel to head down to the study. She knew it was recess at school, so took advantage of the opportunity and called his mobile.

Marco answered with genuine enthusiasm in his voice. 'Gabriella! What a wonderful surprise! I've been thinking of you so much recently. How are you?'

'I'm doing great. Thank you, Marco.' She stifled a small giggle. 'I'm still battling to call you that, and not Mr Carrera.'

'Well, it's about time you got used to it. So, what's new? Have they managed to catch that evil swine who killed our stunning Leigh? It's been very quiet on the Western Front. Just a couple of days ago, I saw Shelagh as I was driving past, but didn't have enough time to stop and catch up with her. You know me: always a deadline to meet and never enough time in a day.'

'No. Unfortunately, I don't have any news about Leigh,' Gabriella said, feeling a tear trickle down her cheek. 'Oh, I miss her terribly. I still can't get my head around the fact that I'll never see her again. It upsets me talking about it. God, why did it have to be Leigh? Can we rather discuss why I'm calling you, Marco?'

'I'm sorry, Gabriella. Please, go on.'

She paused and swallowed nervously. 'I've been invited to the governor's ball, and I wondered if you'd kindly be my escort. I wouldn't feel comfortable with anyone else.' She burst out laughing. 'Gosh, I feel like a schoolgirl again.'

'Ah, what an honour you've bestowed upon me! My goodness, I'm truly touched. I'd love to be your escort for the evening. Rubbing shoulders with the rich and famous won't hurt either now, will it?'

'Great! I'll call you later with more details. Maybe you can also give me a few pointers for my speech?' Gabriella replied cheekily, already knowing his answer.

'That would be my pleasure. I must go, Gabriella – class is about to resume. We'll talk later, though.'

All right, then, Gabriella thought, as she put the landline down. *That's done and dusted. Now all I need to worry about is what to wear!*

As Gabriella strolled down the passage towards her walk-in robe, reflecting on the impending occasion, the landline jangled disruptively behind her.

'Good morning,' came a familiar voice, full of authority.

'Ah, good morning, Lieutenant Ryan. It's lovely to hear from you!' Gabriella responded buoyantly, leaning against the study wall. Speaking to Craig had always had a reassuring effect on her, even over the phone.

'How does it feel to be the toast of Champaign?' he quipped.

'I'm still adjusting to it,' she said, chuckling. 'Thank you for the compliment, though.'

'You've earned it. Congrats!'

'Thanks, Lieutenant. Any updates on the case?'

'Hmm… are you busy at the moment?'

'I always have time for you. Don't hesitate to ask me anything.'

'Excellent. I won't keep you long. I have a simple question: Do you happen to possess the contact information of the upper crust Leigh may have had dealings with?'

Gabriella considered this, fiddling with the landline's cord. 'How about I swing by your office before lunch, and we peruse the list together? Leigh, Ana, and I all shared numerous contacts, so there's no telling what we might uncover.'

'Perfect! I'll see you shortly, Gabriella.'

+ + +

Later that afternoon, an elderly couple struggled to move forward as a gusty wind relentlessly pushed against them. The ferocious air blew through the towering pine trees, triggering the playfulness of their two Dalmatian puppies. The little paws of the black and white pups danced on the dry leaves. The grey-haired woman and her husband held onto their furry companions with all their might, the man tightly gripping his spectacles in his other hand. If they'd known the weather would shift so dramatically, they would never have ventured out with their beloved dogs.

The gleam of sunlight on a reflective object piqued their interest. The tinier pooch scampered right towards it. The woman pursued her with poise, then delicately scooped up a cufflink. Unaware of the importance of their discovery, the couple opted to surrender it to the authorities. They didn't anticipate being ushered directly to the office of a lieutenant.

Craig inquired if they'd discovered the object near the ravine. The woman confirmed it, and her husband added that they'd wanted to bring it in because it must have sentimental value to someone.

Craig inspected the cufflink and focused on the emblem of an embossed *heartagram*. It'd been found close to the location of Leigh's crime scene, so he wondered if this was more than a coincidence. However, he kept this idea to himself.

I'll keep this under wraps, he thought. *It could be our ace in the hole.*

Chapter 18

With Chad now struck off the suspect list, and all known offenders accounted for and questioned, Craig was feeling a little confined in his investigation. The return of the cufflink from Forensics was taking forever, or so it felt, although it had only been three days.

'They gotta come up with something. There must be a print on it. For fuck's sake – a hand is used when putting them on!' He slammed his fist on the desk, then his door flew open. In walked Kirsten.

'Craigie-boy, any newsworthy material at your disposal?' she asked, as she adjusted her cardigan over her shoulders.

'Nothing,' he snapped.

'What's climbed up your ass today?' she said, then covered her mouth. 'You bring out the worst in me when you're so discourteous.' Huffing, she shook her finger at him. 'I've come here out of the goodness of my heart to assist you, but obviously my support is not required. I'll be on my merry way. Goodbye, you ungrateful beast.' She picked up her handbag and turned towards the door.

'I'm sorry, Kirst. You caught me at a bad time. Every time I think there's a glimmer of hope with a new lead, I hit a brick wall again. Please accept my humblest apology for being short with you. Why don't you sit down, and I'll get us coffee?'

She always knew what to say to him when she wanted her way. 'Pure womanly genius is all I can say,' she mumbled under her breath, flashing a cheeky grin.

While they were deep in conversation, hashing out every aspect of the case, there was a familiar knock at the door. Without hesitation, Craig shouted, 'Come on in, Whoopi.'

Coco and Kirsten didn't quite see eye to eye. Kirsten found her brash, and Coco loathed Kirsten's 'ass don't stink' attitude. Her jovial demeanour switched off like a light the moment she laid eyes on Kirsten. The tension was so thick, it could've been sliced with a butterknife.

Coco got in first with a very sarcastic, 'Good day, Your Highness.'

Kirsten rolled her eyes, lips pressed tightly together. 'Your condescension rolls off you like a fog, and it's oh so terribly sad. What's your actual deal, huh?'

'Yo girl, shake ya tail with ya fancy English words. I ain't here for no tea and scones; I came to see my boy, the one and only Lieut, if ya don't mind.' Coco clicked her fingers.

Craig witnessed this in fits of laughter. They both had such huge egos they deserved their own zip codes!

As Kirsten excused herself to go to the bathroom, Coco sat down and handed Craig a package. 'Aside from them ol' timer's prints, we managed to lift a third print, but regrettably, it's not of good quality.'

'How bad is it, Whoops?' Craig asked, running his hands through his hair.

'You want me to try again, boss?' Coco offered, a renewed enthusiasm in her voice. 'I want this prick as much as y'all. I'll get onto it right away.'

The opening of the door instantly changed the mood. Kirsten entered the room and spotted something shiny on the desk. Without blinking, Craig removed it.

'Am I interrupting something?' Kirsten hissed.

'Of course not.'

'Then what do you have in your hand, Craig?' Crossing her arms, Kirsten narrowed her eyes.

'It's nothing, Kirst.'

'I wasn't born yesterday. Show me what you have or I'm out of here.' She took a step towards the door.

'Alright then, Miss Priss.' Craig vigorously shook his head, neck veins throbbing. 'I'll show you, but God help you if you breathe a word of this to anyone. No one knows we have this, except for the elderly couple who found it, Whoopi, and me. I made the decision not to make this common knowledge – at least for now. I'm going against all protocol here, including you in on this confidential and highly sensitive information. My bloody job is on the line if anything leaks out!'

He walked to his whiteboard, leaving the wrapped cufflink on the desk. Kirsten picked it up and took a good look at it.

'I've seen this before,' she said in a small voice.

'*What?*' both Coco and Craig yelled.

'I know I have. I remember the emblem.' She bit her lip, her face crumpling, and put it back down. 'But I can't for the life of me remember where!'

'Go figure,' Coco said, raising her eyebrows. She scooped up the cufflink. 'Let me get back to the lab and stir up some magic.'

'Remember there's a clock on this, Whoopster.'

'Yeah, yeah. Is the Pope Catholic?' She giggled and closed the door behind her.

'I can't stand that woman,' Kirsten said.

She slumped back into her chair and clasped her hands over her face. Her recollection was typically flawless, akin to an elephant's; however, on this occasion, it had let her down. 'I can't recall where I saw that cufflink, Craig, but it definitely wasn't that long ago – possibly a few weeks, or a month at most. The perpetrator is close by.'

Chapter 19

'*Mia bella bambina*,' Francesca said, for the hundredth time since her daughter had returned a fortnight ago, kissing Gabriella on the forehead and warmly embracing her. 'Mama and Papa very proud of you.'

'Thank you, Mama,' Gabriella replied. Tears of joy had left mascara smudged beneath Francesca's eyes, and Gabriella reached out to gently wipe her mother's face. 'I'm just so ecstatic to be able to share this with my amazing, loving family – so much more than you could ever know.'

'Your brothers all come, *si*: Leonardo today evening, Franco tomorrow, Adriano tomorrow evening and my *caro* Alessandro on way with Papa from *aeroporto*,' Francesca said. There was a wide Cheshire-cat smile on her face that said she was absolutely thrilled at the prospect of her children being together under one roof again – and what better roof than hers?

As they walked into the lounge, they heard the car pull up into the driveway. Without hesitating, they both ran outside to greet Alessandro and Pepe. Just under two years apart in age, Gabriella and Alessandro were exceptionally close. They'd basically grown up as twins and formed a special bond over the years.

While they all went inside to unpack and have a welcome cup of tea, a shadow lurked in the background.

'My, my, the party's getting started,' he whispered. 'Look how she hugs him – it's her brother, for shit's sake! What's wrong with this girl? If I hear it's the Italian charm one more time, I'm gonna toss my cookies! Bring me a bucket!'

Sniggering to himself, he flicked his fingers through his hair, removing a few stray leaves shed by the hedge he was hiding behind. 'Well, enough of this. No time to take my eye off the ball – I've already been far too preoccupied these days. Craigie is in dire need of another letter, methinks. Let's go and play editor.'

He got into his car. 'Oh dear, what a conundrum! Another inextricable situation for you, Lieutenant… Now, now, maintain that focus, Rip. Remember our aim. We gotta get that head of his to spin around three hundred and sixty degrees without stopping. Yeah, like a dive bomber. Ooh, I like it!'

A little while later, he was in his home office, brainstorming ideas for his upcoming letter. Alphabetical characters cut from paper were scattered all over his desk. With a glue stick at the ready, he worked through his assembly line, making progress at a steady pace.

He paused briefly, then stepped back to admire his handiwork. Curled finger pressed against his lips, he inhaled deeply and marvelled at his own brilliance. At this point, he knew he was unstoppable, invincible, and capable of achieving anything. His right foot landed on an empty crate, which would do as his soapbox. With a piercing cry that sent shivers down his spine, he pumped his fist. 'This should send them into overdrive!'

He had other things he needed to do. Places to be. First, he had to decide on his attire.

'I reckon I need to make a statement tonight. Hmm, best I spruce myself up like a celeb. Only the best, right?' He rummaged through his bowtie collection. 'Damn, did I get my Givenchy tux back from the cleaners? This is an extraordinary event – yes, I think I'll wear my precious cufflinks.'

+ + +

Gabriella didn't want to alarm her family, but something was bothering her. Everywhere she went, she saw

Sebastian Hampton. This local 'bad boy', known around town for his antics, seemed to be stalking her.

Sebastian had a weakness for women. Especially the pretty ones. Gabriella knew that he'd harboured a crush on her for years; since sixth grade, in fact. The girls liked him, but his extreme shyness kept them at bay. He would avoid all of them at any cost, much to their disappointment. All of them except Gabriella.

The only time he and Gabriella had ever really talked was in drama class. He'd been able to take on the role of any character he was given; it was like he slipped into another skin. He was a natural, and a fantastic scene partner. Gabriella had thought that he could be a wonderful friend too – maybe something more. But no matter how much she'd tried to engage with him outside of the classroom, he wouldn't meet her eyes or say a word. He'd just follow her from a distance, always in the corner of her vision.

After graduation, his life took a turn for the worse. He got involved with drugs and alcohol, earning himself a bad reputation. He had numerous brushes with the law and spent a while in prison, for charges unknown. There were rumours, of course. Some said he'd been dealing drugs, while others whispered that he was done in for drunk driving or that he'd finally snapped and killed someone. His parents, his girlfriend – or boyfriend – a rival gang member; the story changed depending on who you were talking to.

One thing was for certain: he'd been Gabriella's shadow on and off over the years, and it looked like he was back to his old ways, inspired by the mania that had overtaken Champaign in the wake of her Oscar win.

Even though he was a good-looking man, she'd noticed he was rather unkempt these days. She couldn't recall his hair ever being so dirty and matted. That scruffy, unshaven beard did nothing for him either.

Gabriella contemplated telling Alessandro about her suspicions. He'd always been the one to tell Sebastian to back off when things got a little too intense; he was the one she could always count on.

No, she decided. *I don't want to worry him yet.* It had been so long since the family was all together – she didn't want to ruin that. She'd tell him a little later when everything had calmed down.

+ + +

Back at the station, Cody knocked on Craig's office door and entered without waiting for an invitation.

'You got another love letter, Lieut,' Cody said, passing over the glue-stained envelope. Craig ripped it open. True to form, in bold black cut-out letters, there was the killer's latest message.

WE MADE A PACT TO ACT, THAT'S A FACT ~

'Fuck, this asshole is really getting on my nerves.' Craig grimaced. 'I'm over these letters. Cody, call up the university and get one of the criminologists down here, pronto. We gotta get into this prick's mInd.'

He stared at the words, reading them repeatedly. The word *act* suddenly became clear.

'Wait,' he said. Cody stopped in his tracks. 'Who's synonymous with acting in this city?'

Cody gasped. 'Gabriella Cantrello?'

'Exactly! She could be in danger,' Craig said. The words were barely out of his mouth before he was grabbing his coat and car keys. 'Cody, make the criminologist's appointment for two hours from now.'

Ten minutes later, Alessandro Cantrello opened the door to an out-of-breath Craig. 'Can I help you?'

'I'm Lieutenant Ryan,' Craig said, sticking his hand out. 'Is Gabriella here?'

'Alessandro,' he replied. 'It's nice to finally meet you. My sister's upstairs. Please, come inside and I will call her.'

He showed Craig into the living room, gesturing for him to sit down. 'Can I get you anything? Coffee?'

'No thanks. I just need to speak to Gabriella.'

Alessandro disappeared down the hall, calling out his sister's name. A few moments later, she came bouncing into the room, as beautiful as ever.

God, she looks so happy, Craig thought. *I don't want to frighten her.*

'Good morning, Lieutenant! This is a wonderful surprise.' She sat down on the elegant white sofa and crossed her legs in a ladylike manner.

'Unfortunately, this isn't a social call. We're intensifying our search and broadening our angles on this investigation. For this to be effective, we need the names of all your acquaintances, business and personal. The same procedure will be applied to Anastasia. You don't need to be alarmed. This is purely a cautionary measure to cover all bases with you girls.' He leaned forward. 'Please, Gabriella, if you recall any incidents from the past couple of years – disagreements with or jealous outbursts from friends or co-stars, regardless of how trivial they may have been – we need to know. We need those names. Does anyone come to mind?'

Gabriella glanced around the otherwise empty room. 'Lieutenant, I honestly think Sebastian Hampton is stalking me. Everywhere I go, he's either there or nearby. I've known him virtually my entire life, and, well, he used to follow me around sometimes, show up at the places I would frequent – I think he was trying to work up the courage to talk to me. He was mostly harmless back then. I would never have placed him in the *creepy* category. But this time... it feels different. He stands and stares with absolutely no expression. Do you understand what I'm saying? It's like he's boring holes into my body. Thank God, he hasn't approached me or done anything to harm me. But, Lieutenant, I'm scared, and I don't know what to do.' Almost out of breath, she stifled a sob.

'So, let me get this straight,' Craig said, 'he's never performed any violent act towards you? It'll obviously be difficult to pull him in for questioning without any evidence but let me see what I can do.' He paused, then added, sotto voce: 'May I ask why you looked around before you started telling me this, Gabriella?'

'I just don't want to raise any suspicions with my family. I'll tell Alessandro, but Mama and Papa? They'd freak out.' She shrugged. 'I didn't want to overreact and earn the reputation of being a drama queen or diva.'

'Do you feel unsafe, Gabriella?'

She hesitated. 'I honestly don't think he would do anything to harm me. Maybe we just need to monitor the situation, as awkward as it may seem?'

'Of course. Thank you for sharing with me – I greatly appreciate it. This is good to know.' Craig stood up and shook her hand.

Out of nowhere, Francesca came pounding into the room. 'Good morning, my dear *signor*. How are you?' she asked, wiping at her eyeliner.

'All good, thank you, Mrs Cantrello. I was just leaving, as your lovely daughter has answered all my annoying questions as efficiently as always.' He chuckled, already walking towards the door, fully aware of what was about to happen.

'No, no, no, no, Lieutenant. You knowing better.' She shook her finger in Craig's direction. 'No coming in Cantrello house and no eat food. *Si vergognino* for no invite you to lunch. *Vieni con me mia bella*, Gabriella.'

Craig used all his powers of persuasion to induce Francesca to let him off the hook. The station required his presence now, not later. Right now! His meeting with the criminologist in an hour was his saving grace. He felt relieved – albeit a tad embarrassed – after successfully pulling rank on Francesca, but it being Friday, things couldn't wait until Monday morning.

During his journey back to the station, Craig pondered the progress of his investigation. He was beginning to feel trapped in his conventional approach. He needed to shake things up, but how?

I need another brain to pick. One totally unrelated to the case, with a fresh take, to re-examine all the aspects.

The most recent letter had triggered a wave of fear that travelled through his entire body. He was certain that another killing was in the works. He needed to prevent it before it was too late, but at this point, he was grasping at straws.

His shoulders sagged under the weight of his frustration. He muttered, '*We shall never surrender!*' and suddenly beamed as he pictured Winston Churchill puffing on his cigar.

The moment he arrived at the station, Craig mobilised his team and began implementing a plan to place Sebastian under surveillance. This would prove challenging; as rumour had it, he was currently homeless. Craig assigned two of his officers, Pierre, and Wesley, to go undercover on Branston Avenue, where Sebastian had last been sighted. It was a rough area of town where the less-than-savoury characters of Champaign congregated, so the situation could escalate quickly. Despite the potential danger, the pair were eager to undertake the mission, being both highly trained and skilled. Craig dismissed them early from duty so they could prepare for their task.

Soon after, criminologist Connor Lincoln strode into the police precinct, clutching a steaming cup of java as he made a beeline for Craig's office. He rapped on the door and barged in.

Eyebrows raised, Craig looked up from his computer. Connor leaned against his desk with a small smile playing at his lips. 'Good morning, Lieut,' he said, raising his hand in a playful salute. 'How's things? I'm guessing this ain't a social call, right?'

'I need to pick your brain. Just a warning – it's a tricky one.'

Connor tilted his head. 'Oh, really? Go ahead and try me. I'm up for a challenge. Hey, I get paid by the university to be at your beck and call. If it takes a couple of months, so be it.'

'Jeezus, Connor, we don't have months. We gotta solve this case as soon as possible. Check this out.' Rising to his feet, he proceeded confidently towards the whiteboard on the wall, Connor right behind him. 'As you can see from this section in blue, the lab's ascertained that fibres from a purple rug and a long-haired dog were found at Leigh's crime scene.'

'What did the ERT come up with?' Connor asked, examining the tangled web of colourful writing, circled words, arrows, and question marks.

'Nothing constructive to date. We've been close many a time, but still no cigar.' Craig took a step back. 'Okay. Let's rehash these points in green. These are the lab's first batch of results from testing the prints on the cufflink.'

Connor swiped ferociously on his iPad, compiling statistical data of his own. 'Give me a moment to make a mental adjustment, then I'll be all ears.'

Craig stared intently at the whiteboard, waiting not-so-patiently for Connor. As he considered various theories, he heard the shuffling of feet behind him. Turning around, he saw two of his colleagues, Cody, and Skye, barging into the room.

'Guys, what's going on?' he asked, perplexed.

'We just got an update from HQ,' Cody replied breathlessly. 'A witness saw a long-haired dog near the crime scene.'

Craig's mind raced as he absorbed this new information. 'Both of you, head out to the neighbourhood and inquire if anyone observed anything suspicious,' he barked, picking up the phone. 'I'm going to call Coco and see whether she has anything more specific on the breed, or any news on the cufflink.'

As Craig waited for Coco to answer, unease lingered as he sensed the puzzle pieces slowly aligning, realizing he had a considerable distance to cover before unravelling the complexities of this case. Determination swelling in his chest, he steeled himself for what lay ahead. The hunt had just gotten even more intense.

+   +   +

Pierre and Wesley took to their new roles like ducks to water, arriving on Branston Avenue late that afternoon and blending in quickly with its other residents. They never lost sight of the fact that gate crashers didn't generally get an easy ride. It was a dog-eat-dog world out there, so all they had to do was watch each other's backs. Nothing novel about it; they'd been partners since graduating from the academy and knew each other's strengths and weaknesses.

Their focus was real, palpable. It was almost as if they'd been fitted with blinkers, shutting out any distractions. They were like two racehorses in the starting gates, waiting for the signal to unleash their full potential – and when that signal came, their professionalism and training kicked in automatically. As the sun fell, they began to ask questions about Sebastian, their voices even and calm. As they delved deeper into his life, they had to shield each other from suspicion. It was a delicate dance, a game of cat and mouse. But they were champs, and they played it with finesse.

Consensus on the street was that Sebastian was a solitary figure, preferring to sit on his tattered rug, smoking, and drinking, lost in his own thoughts. His sole preoccupation was with finding his next fix, which he pursued with the fervour of a zealot. He resembled a living, breathing corflute sign advertising the local bottle store, as he made his way in and out of the establishment at least six times a day. There had been a few run-ins with some of the unsavoury drug dealers in the area, and more recently, a stabbing. Though Sebastian had been questioned, no one knew what came of it. Wesley and Pierre persisted in their investigation, leaving no stone unturned.

+ + +

Meanwhile, Rip frantically searched for his cufflinks.

'I know I put them in this case.' He almost scratched his head off, then closed his eyes, trying to backtrack his movements. Totally frustrated, he spun around in his closet, looking in every direction. 'They've got to be here! I always put them back in their place! When was the last time I wore them?'

His voice quavered with rage. As he rummaged through his closet, throwing clothes and shoes in every direction, his frustration reached boiling point. His cufflinks, the missing piece of his attire, were nowhere to be found. Where on earth were they? Had they been swiped? Or did he lend them to someone? His thoughts were a complete void.

However, the day he'd been presented with them was permanently etched in his memory, as vivid as a polished diamond. As if it were that moment again, he could hear the mantras of the powers that be rolling around in his head, exciting him to new levels of darkness and reconfirming what ignited the devil within the deepest, darkest part of his soul. This sense of entitlement caused him to ponder over his forthcoming soiree with Victim Number Two.

'The challenge is to keep the momentum going,' he sang. 'I gotta get this ball a-rollin'.'

Chapter 20

Gabriella stepped into the room, and her mother gasped in admiration of her beauty. She wore a breathtaking Valentino dress that hugged her curves in all the right places. Its fiery red hue emphasised her confidence and boldness, and its intricate beading shimmered in the light, adding to her allure. But what really completed the look was the stunning hat that rested on Gabriella's perfectly coiffed hair. The hat, crafted by the renowned Italian milliner Federica Moretti, was a nod to classical fashion, with its wide brim and structured shape.

'I'm going Italian tonight, Mama!' she said, as she tilted her hat a little more to the side. 'Do you think I could take the runways of Milan by storm?'

'Ah, *mia bella, Italia il mio bel paese, e il migliore al mondo* for haute couture,' Francesca said, voice thick with longing for her beloved homeland.

Gabriella's fingers trembled as she ran them over the intricate bevelled edges of her handcrafted full-length mirror. She'd been so confident that the hat would add an extra touch of sophistication to her outfit, but now she wasn't so sure. With a heavy sigh, she moved her face from side to side, scrutinising every inch of herself in the mirror. Finally, she reached up and delicately removed the hat from her head. As she smoothed down her hair, Gabriella knew that she'd made the right choice. Maintaining proper etiquette was always more important than trying to stand out, especially in high society.

Meanwhile, in another part of town, Marco stood tall and proud in his Gianfranco Ferré suit. He loved the feeling of the smooth, expensive fabric against his skin, and he couldn't wait to show it off to the Hollywood elite. For Marco, this was more than just a party. It was a chance to live out his dreams, to bask in the glamour and glitz of Tinseltown, the reason he'd gotten into drama in the first place. He checked the time on his gleaming Rolex and grinned, feeling a surge of excitement in his chest.

I can't be late picking up Gabriella, so best I leave now and make allowances for the traffic.

He picked up his keys and headed towards the garage. Sure enough, the roads were packed; the entirety of Champaign's elite was on their way to the ball.

Finally, his red Lamborghini Countach pulled up at the Cantrello home. As he made his way up the pathway, he was met by a man with a frosty set to his features.

'Good evening. Mr Carrera, I presume?'

'And which of Gabriella's highly regarded brothers would you be, young man?' Marco asked, taken aback by the coolness of this unknown individual.

'I'm Alessandro, Gabriella's favourite – and most protective – brother. Anyone other than Bjorn escorting my sister will be put through his paces. One thing is for sure, Mr Carrera: the Spanish Inquisition has nothing on this family.' He firmly gripped Marco's shoulder. 'I know you aren't her partner, per se. However, Bjorn would expect nothing less from me. Especially with Gabriella's new status. So, on that note, please do come in.'

Alessandro opened the front door and swung his arm, beckoning Marco inside. 'I'll see if Gabriella is ready. Please take a seat in the living room. I'll be right back.'

Marco made himself comfortable on the couch. As he sat back, he noticed a photograph of him and all three of his girls taken at their graduation.

God, they were so young. So beautiful. Leigh...

He got up to take a closer look, and as he stepped forward towards the mantlepiece, Gabriella entered the room. Marco turned to face her and gasped, taken aback by her enchanting beauty.

'Wow, Gabriella... I'm at a loss for words. To say you look exquisite is quite the understatement.'

'Why thank you,' Gabriella replied, as she felt herself blushing from the compliment. 'Shall we be on our way?'

'Well, that depends,' Marco said, turning to Alessandro. 'Did I pass the test?'

Alessandro gave him a frown. 'I don't know...'

Gabriella elbowed her brother. 'Stop teasing, Al.'

His face quickly morphed into a smile; he never could refuse her. He offered Marco his hand. 'I suppose you'll be a suitable companion for the evening. Take care of my sister, yes?'

'Of course,' Marco said. And with that, the two of them were off. Alessandro was joined by Pepe and Francesca, waving to Gabriella from the doorway as she and Marco disappeared into the night.

The pair could see the lights from the event all the way down the other end of the tree-lined street. Between the other cars and the people mingling about, they inched their way there. Gabriella ducked her head down, trying to hide her face from any onlookers outside the window.

'I don't know if I can do this, Marco,' she said, on the verge of panic. 'Acting… well, it's all make-believe. If I mess up, I can always do another take. But this… I'm not who they think I am. I'm just a girl, not some glamorous figure.'

He took one hand off the wheel to clutch her hand; he could feel her trembling. 'You're going to be great,' he said softly. 'I have faith in you.'

'Well, at least one of us does,' she said with a half-hearted laugh.

'Have I ever steered you wrong?'

'No,' she said. 'But–'

'No buts.' They were almost at the building. The flash of cameras as the governor and his wife arrived just ahead of them was almost blinding. 'And no fear. This is the part of a lifetime: Gabriella Cantrello, beloved actress, daughter, sister, and friend. That's all you must be tonight.

Whatever you do, it will be perfect, because it is you who's doing it.'

She sighed. 'You're saying I should play myself?'

'Doesn't everyone? You remember the concept of the persona?'

'Yes.' She nodded, then took a deep breath. 'Okay. I can do that. I can be myself.'

He gave her a gentle smile as the car crawled to a stop and he stepped outside. He handed the keys to the chauffeur and went around to open Gabriella's door, offering her his hand.

'Shall we?'

She reached out and took it.

The governor's soiree was held in a beautiful ballroom just west of the university campus. Gabriella had attended a few weddings and functions here in the past, but upon seeing all the glitz and glam that had been brought out for the big event, she was stunned. It was a large room, spacious enough for a stage, dozens of white-clothed tables, and countless people milling about and mingling – and, of course, there was still plenty of room to dance! The floor-to-ceiling windows were adorned with billowing gossamer curtains, letting in the soft glow of moonlight, which only added to the ethereal nature of the space. There were white roses and candles everywhere, their flames reflecting off Gabriella's dress, making her shine. As they entered the ballroom, all heads turned in her direction.

'They're all staring at me,' she whispered.

'Of course they are. You're beautiful.'

She and Marco danced for some time, gracefully gliding across the maple dance floor. It didn't last forever; Gabriella was one of the most coveted partners of the evening, and after two hours or so, she was sure she'd been taken for a spin by nearly every man there.

'So, who is the man accompanying you this evening, Ms Cantrello?' her current dance partner asked. 'I couldn't help but notice that your fiancé was not in attendance.'

She recognised his face. Michael Morales was a young and successful Chicago businessman, interested in expanding across the state and beyond. Exactly the calibre of person the governor was hoping to appeal to.

'Marco is a dear friend of mine, and a devoted patron of the arts. Seeing as Bjorn is out of the country now, I extended the invitation.'

'How kind of you,' he said, twirling her.

'Mind if I cut in?' Gabriella heard Marco ask. 'Gabriella, the governor wants you up on stage soon.'

Her heart skipped a beat. 'Already?'

'I know. Time just flies when you're having fun, doesn't it?'

'We could just slip out. I'm sure no one would notice.'

'Besides the whole guest list?' Marco retorted. 'That's not the Gabriella I know. You never run from a challenge.'

She sighed, shaking her head. 'Why do you have to be so sensible?'

'Years of practice,' he said with a smirk, squeezing her hand. 'Now go. Knock 'em dead.'

Gabriella walked up to the stage. The room fell silent. She locked eyes with Marco. He gave her a slight nod. She remembered the advice he'd given while helping her with the speech.

Pretend I'm the only one in the room, Gabriella. You're talking to a friend. Simple, right?

She took a deep breath and put on her biggest 'celebrity' smile. 'Hello, everyone. How are we all this evening?' She was met with a wave of warm murmurs. She steeled herself and pressed forward. 'I'd like to welcome you all to the annual Governor's Ball. It's an honour to have you here, in our lovely city – even more so to be invited as a guest of honour to speak with you tonight. I've lived in Champaign most of my life, and I'm proud to call this extraordinary place my home.'

If you were to ask Gabriella what she talked about for the next twenty minutes, she wouldn't be able to tell you. She knew what she'd rehearsed in her bathroom mirror for hours, and what Marco had helped her painstakingly craft, but now? Words flowed from her mouth without a thought, passionate and natural. Certainly off-script.

Marco was right. She just had to be herself.

Before she knew it, the room was erupting into applause. She blinked. Was it over already? As she stepped off the stage, and the governor started his address, Marco wrapped her in a big hug.

'I knew you could do it!'

'How'd I do?'

'Beautifully,' he said with a wide grin. They looked back up at the stage. 'How about a nightcap? You want to get out of here?'

'Oh, God yes,' she said, laughing.

They slipped out of the ballroom and headed down to Cloud Nine, a vibey pub at Champaign Country Club.

'A toast,' Marco said, leaning forward and clinking his glass with Gabriella's. 'To your courage. And to many more years of success.'

'To the teacher who has so many little nuggets of wisdom still tucked away, which he's kind enough to share,' she said in return. 'Seriously, Marco… thank you. I couldn't have done it without you.'

He waved her off, shaking his head. 'Of course you could have. But I'm always happy to be of service. You know I'd do anything for you girls.'

Marco, a perfect gentleman, returned Gabriella home shortly after. He shook hands with Alessandro and accepted Francesca's offer to come for dinner the following weekend.

With another hug from Gabriella, thanking him yet again, he was off.

The ball was a great success, and as fundraisers go, it exceeded all expectations. The following morning, photos of Gabriella, Marco, the governor, his wife, and numerous other dignitaries were splashed all over the local broadsheets and tabloids.

+ + +

Back on Branston Avenue, Pierre and Wesley had made progress with Sebastian over the past few days and were invited into his makeshift shack further down the road. As they sat on the cold concrete of the sidewalk, Wesley noticed a half-cut, threadbare rug with missing tassels. A purple rug.

He signalled to Pierre to keep Sebastian occupied while he carefully removed a fibre from the rug for the lab and took a photo for possible evidence.

'So, how long have you been here, Seb?' Pierre asked.

'A while,' Sebastian frowned. 'Pretty much right out of high school. Made some bad choices, trusted the wrong people, and things kept snowballing from there. Not exactly a line of people willing to take a chance on me now. My old man's been dead for fifteen years, and my mom… well, less said about her, the better.'

'Shit, man. I'm sorry.'

He shrugged. 'It is what it is. We must live with our choices. You're learning that now, aren't you?'

Pierre agreed, though somewhat sombrely. 'I know what you mean.'

'Look, I hate to be the bearer of bad news,' Sebastian said. 'I'd love to tell you that everything's going to work out fine for you, but honestly? Things will get worse the longer you stay. I've seen it time and time again. Once you're out here, it gets harder and harder to get back on the right track. People don't see you as a person anymore. They throw you from one bad spot to the next.' He sniffed. 'You seem like nice folks. I hope the two of you can still get back on your feet. Stay away from the drugs and shit if you can. It helps.'

Sebastian sat down and threw some pieces of newspaper into an old sawn-off 44-gallon drum. He took out a battered lighter and managed to get a spark, sticking his hands over the small flame, and letting the warmth seep into his fingers. They sat in silence.

A few moments later, a scrawny Irish setter came strolling by. Sebastian's face lit up.

'Come on in, Paddy! Come here,' he said, lowering himself onto his haunches as he beckoned the dog. 'That's a good boy. Where have you been all day, huh? Patrolling the streets, I suppose. My brave boy.' Sebastian lovingly stroked Paddy and ruffled his ears. Paddy wagged his tail, then departed to the next group.

'Is that your dog?' Pierre asked.

'No, but he might as well be. I'm the only one who feeds him, poor thing.'

'Does he ever sleep in here?'

He shrugged. 'Sometimes. All depends on his mood and who his flavour of the day is.'

Pierre and Wesley simultaneously looked at each other, realising they were thinking the same thing. Purple rug, long-haired dog: could this be the breakthrough they had so desperately been waiting for?

Chapter 21

Gabriella basked in the warmth and laughter of her family. Her siblings surrounded her, giggling and munching on their favourite snacks. Their mother bustled about the kitchen, humming a happy tune as she whipped up their favourite dishes, relishing that all her babies were home with her for the first time in ten years. It was crystal clear that she was one content mama!

The scent of garlic and tomatoes wafted through the air, mingling with the fragrant bouquet of fresh flowers that graced the table. Gabriella breathed deeply, savouring the heady mixture of aromas. Her stomach growled with anticipation as she waited for her mother's culinary creations to emerge from the oven.

At last, the door swung open, and Francesca emerged, bearing a platter of steaming lasagne. Her children whooped with delight. While they ate, they chatted and laughed, trading stories and memories that spanned the past decade. It was clear that this was more than just a family dinner – it was a long-overdue reunion, a chance to reconnect and revel in the bonds that bound them together. As Gabriella savoured the love that infused every bite of the delicious, cheesy pasta, she felt her heart swell with gratitude and joy. It was moments like these that made life worth living, that reminded her of the deep affection that anchored her to her family. And as they lingered over dessert, sharing stories and jokes late into the night, she knew this was a memory that she'd treasure for years to come.

+ + +

Rip had given up his search for his cufflinks, having failed to find them after looking in every single nook and cranny of his home, including the garden and outbuildings.

'Ah, what the hell – no time to waste crying over spilled milk,' he said. 'I need to execute the next segment of my plan. Tonight, tomorrow night, to be or not to be, that is the question.' He chortled at this execrable blend of his and Shakespeare's soliloquies.

While he paced up and down as if he were in the middle of a one-acter, it suddenly dawned on him that he needed a theatrical approach to his next rendezvous.

'What better venue than the historic Virginia Theatre? With her recent restoration to her former glory, she's the perfect setting. I'll make my own 1920s silent movie!'

His thoughts drifted in his warped mind, setting his vivid plan into action.

'We'll have an incredible night together and go back to my place for a nightcap,' he muttered. 'With all the hype surrounding her visit, she'll revel in the quiet warmth of my home, ha ha! It won't take her long to realise there's a spark between us. In that moment, it will ignite, and before she knows what's happening, we'll be making passionate love on the Montage rug in front of the fireplace.'

At this point, he had one thing in mind. His libido superseded all rationality; he started jerking himself off, just thinking about the dominance he'd soon have over his victim.

'This will be romance personified for her. There'll be candles all over the living room, dining room and bedroom – even rose petals leading to my bed from the dimly-lit guest bathroom. Dinner will be in the oven and long-stemmed roses on the dining room table. Yes, I can live with this, being the incurable romantic that I am.'

Rip snorted at his own little joke.

'After the entrée at the fireplace, we'll proceed to the kitchen, à la *Fatal Attraction*. I'll take another peek at her well-toned torso, then wrap my legs around that voluptuous body, pinning her down as I enter her with great vigour. Maybe I'll hold a meat cleaver in one hand for an extra little jab. A few more strokes, then I'll turn her over and work my tongue down the contour of her back, making my way down the finely paved expressway to her sexy ass.'

Licking his lips, he allowed his head to fall back as he lost himself further in fantasy.

'We'll walk naked into the dining room; I'll be a flawless gentleman and seat her to be waited on. Then... *poof!* I'll disappear into the kitchen and return with the first course, dressed only in my apron, pitching a tent with my hard-on. Sex between courses will be on the menu, then we'll end with dessert served all over our bodies. Yum, I can't wait! Then off to the bedroom to continue in comfort amidst the petals and candlelight. This forbidden fruit will be a climax of its own.'

A slow smile spread across his face.

'Only after I've shagged her brains out will the dastardly deed be done.'

+ + +

Preparations were underway for a celebration in tribute to Gabriella, organised by her devoted parents, to commemorate her exceptional accomplishments. Her relatives and friends would grace the occasion. It was a remarkable chance for her to reunite with everyone before she resumed her life amidst the glitz and glamour of Hollywood. Her agent had been relentlessly hounding her for weeks, emphasising the need for her to capitalise on her celebrity status in the aftermath of the Oscars; procrastination wasn't an option.

Finally, a fortnight after the governor's gala, everything was in place for the celebration, apart from one thing: Francesca would not hear of caterers coming into her kitchen.

'*Non capisco*,' she said, with a frown on her brow, when her family had the audacity to even suggest that – just for this occasion – she should sit back and relax while other people did the work. 'Francesca no in kitchen? *Assolutamente* no!'

As with every other time she'd entertained, Francesca had everything under control that Saturday evening. Arancini, pesto bruschetta, and her customised cheesy pepperoni bombs had just come out of her large double-door oven, filling the kitchen with the most delicious aroma. These delights were added to the other plates of scrumptious Italian hors d'oeuvres. The boys had been summoned to cart the food out to the entertainment area, where the platters were laid out professionally, ready for the guests' arrival.

'*Ora e il momento di prepararsi per la serata,*' Francesca said, a glowing smile on her face as she listened to the banter between her children. Dutifully, they disappeared to get ready for the night, while Francesca went to her own bathroom and stripped out of her tomato-stained cooking clothes. Pepe had drawn a welcoming bubble bath for her. All she wanted was to look perfect tonight.

For her beloved *bella bambina*, everything would be perfect.

A couple of hours later, the Cantrellos were all spruced up and gathered in the lounge for their *bevanda preferita* – a family tradition – delighting in the fact they were celebrating together.

Soon, the party was in full swing; the who's who in town were there in all their glory. The constant drone of multiple conversations competed with the loud music. Hearty laughter was heard around the entertainment area, trailing into the kitchen and dining room, where more food was available. Francesca pranced around in top form, never seen without a tray in her hands. Pepe was given an authoritative instruction to follow suit, and he executed this effortlessly, as he had for many years.

They make a great team, Gabriella thought, laughing out loud as she watched her parents' antics. Her heart was warmed by all the efforts that everyone went to for her, but she couldn't help the little ache that came from missing Bjorn. She absolutely adored him.

Every so often, one of the family would talk to Gabriella, either reminiscing or telling her how proud they were of her. 'Thank you,' she would say to each one, and she meant it. She still couldn't get over the fact that her hard work and luck had finally paid off. It all felt surreal, but the support of her family meant everything.

By half past midnight, there were just a handful of guests left: the proverbial die-hards. She was sitting on the sofa next to Alessandro, her head on his shoulder, his arm around her. Her stomach was full of all the delicious food her mother had forced down her throat – not literally, of course, but even she wasn't exempt from Francesca's whims.

Her phone rang. She fished it out of her pocket with less grace than normal.

Who could be calling at this hour? Bjorn?

She was barely on the phone for a minute, then hung up. She looked over at her brother. His eyes were shut. She didn't want to wake him, so she slowly lifted her head and slipped out carefully from his embrace. Grabbing a blanket from the back of the sofa, she draped it over him, before giving him a quick peck on his forehead.

'Love ya, sis,' he muttered.

'Love you too,' she said. And, without another word to anyone, Gabriella grabbed her purse and slipped out the door, into the night.

Chapter 22

Rip's plan was playing out to perfection; he couldn't have done it better without writing the script. This beautiful and extraordinary young woman had put up a massive fight, exercising resistance until he'd forced Rohypnol-laced wine down her throat.

'You wanted to drink down, now it's time to live up,' he gloated, slapping her body, which was limp from the drugs and the destructive beatings he'd administered.

Gabriella was floating in and out of consciousness, dazed and not quite comprehending what was happening. He picked her up from his bed. 'Shall we go down to my wine cellar?' he said. 'I believe a toast is in order, to celebrate what we have discovered within ourselves.'

Vaguely, Gabriella focused on the steps leading down to a massive, carved wooden door. This was no cellar; they were on their way to his basement, his den of iniquity.

By now, she was barely breathing. All Rip could hear coming out of her mouth was a faint: *'Mama, Papa...'*

He flicked her mutilated body over an easel and forced himself into her once more, counting every stroke as he viciously penetrated deeper and deeper into this poor, beguiling being. Each time, he recited something more despicable than the last and laughed uncontrollably, knowing it was almost over.

'I have just shown you my power and your passivity. My divine superior force. Now, who exactly is the luminary here? I dismiss rather than discount all irrelevant things. Yes. You and Leigh; together, you both served my gratification. You see, Gabriella dearest, you make it impossible to resist the compulsion when the compulsion comes.'

As he was about to ejaculate, he quickly withdrew, some semen landing on her stomach. Immediately realising his mistake, he wiped her body clean. He struck her on the head with a baseball bat – the most egregious act of all, the deliberate erasure of hope for Gabriella – then relished stabbing her multiple times, switching knives.

'Mama,' she choked out.

'Mama's not coming to save you,' he hissed.

In a single, swift motion, he severed her left earlobe, then knelt down to strangle her with a red scarf, watching the blood pump its way out of her body.

'Do say hi to Leigh for me,' he said, savouring the sound of her final, laboured breath.

+ + +

There was bedlam in the Cantrello home the following morning. The entire family were frantically calling Gabriella's phone, which had been switched off. They had left hundreds of panic-stricken messages.

'*Mia bella*, where is my beautiful Gabriella?' Francesca sobbed uncontrollably. '*Perche* she go and no tell me? *Perche mia bella?*'

Her brothers patrolled the streets, calling as many people as they knew, to no avail.

An hour later, Shelagh and Dylan arrived to offer support to Francesca and Pepe.

'My darlings, we are so sorry,' Shelagh said amidst tears. 'We know exactly what you're going through and are praying for her safe return.'

When Gabriella still hadn't returned by late afternoon, Craig arrived on the scene and immediately started scouring the area, calling for back-up. Within minutes, half the Champaign Police Department were in and around the Cantrello house. After delegating officers to search the area on foot, Craig went on the radio, instructing the station to send out an APB on Gabriella and set up as many roadblocks as possible to all neighbouring states.

What the fuck is happening in this city? he thought, as he chain-smoked. *I'm no further with Leigh's investigation, and now Gabriella's missing. This is a fucking nightmare.*

He blew out the last puff of his cigarette before knocking on the front door. Pepe opened it, his grand old face signifying suffering, not defeat. The pain in his eyes spoke volumes. Craig rested his hand on Pepe's shoulder as they nodded simultaneously, thinking the same thoughts without uttering a word.

Inside, the distressful sound of crying soaked the living room. Craig glanced in the direction of Francesca; the usually larger-than-life character was now a waif-like creature, huddled up on the couch in Alessandro's arms. He brought the family up to speed on what the department was doing to locate Gabriella. Her fiancé, Bjorn, had been notified and was on his way to the airport in Buenos Aires to fly home and join the search for his darling princess.

+   +   +

On the other side of Champaign, Rip had cleaned up everything and was busy preparing Gabriella for her final performance. He'd dressed her up in a renaissance gown with a wasp waist, leg-of-mutton sleeves, and a ruff to hide her cut-off ear at first sight, adding a string of pearls to complement the outfit. He plastered theatrical makeup over her face, accentuating her eyes and lips.

She was ready for the show to commence.

Upon arriving at the theatre under the cover of falling night, he swiftly picked up Gabriella off the back seat of the car and hurried to a side door. To his amazement, it was unlocked. He carried her up the stairs flanking the stage, arranging her over a chair he'd pulled to its centre. Her lifeless body kept slipping down onto the floor, which enraged him. He kicked her furiously and spat in her face.

'What are you doing? That's not in the script!' He kicked her again. 'Listen to me!'

He stopped for a moment and regrouped himself. Realising his mistake, he wiped off his saliva. *Phew, that was close*, he thought. *No time for errors, Rip. Focus!*

He turned and walked backstage to look for something more suitable to place her on. In the back corner, behind an antediluvian screen, he found the perfect Blenheim-leather chesterfield sofa. It was too heavy for one person to lift, so he dragged it along the floor and positioned it in the middle of the stage, replacing the chair.

He picked up Gabriella's body and tactically draped her over the sofa, until she appeared to be set for the first scene in a dramatic play. Delighted with his replication, he stood back to admire his work of art. He contemplated playing a quick piece on the elaborate Wurlitzer pipe organ in front of him. Deciding against it, he turned and bowed, then descended the stairs. He was quite confident it would take a few days for her body to be discovered; there was no daily schedule at the theatre.

+ + +

Gabriella had now been missing for a full day, and the tension at the Cantrello home had amplified. Every single person was playing their part and doing everything humanly possible to locate Gabriella.

Craig pulled Alessandro aside. 'Did Gabriella tell you about Sebastian Hampton?'

Alessandro's face drained of colour. 'She did. You think this is him?'

'What did she tell you?'

'Nothing much – she said she'd talk to me later. She didn't want to ruin the party. That *stronzo*... he's been obsessed with her for years. Can't count the number of times I've had to tell him to back off. I just thought he was a little lost, you know? He didn't seem like the type who would...' He shook his head, eyes welling. 'I should've known.'

Craig immediately excused himself. Sirens roaring, he broke all speed limits on his way to the station. He'd already told Pierre and Wesley to head down to Branston Avenue and get involved in a brawl, making sure Sebastian was involved, which would allow Craig to apprehend him and do some lightweight questioning while he was in custody.

On Craig's arrival at the station, Police Chief Riaan was waiting for him. They went straight to his office, closing the door behind them.

'I know what you're thinking,' Riaan said, swallowing deeply. The concern in his voice was palpable.

'A repeater...'

'Possibly. This is just too much of a coincidence – two of the hottest celebrities in town. We need to delve deeper, Craig. Get to the bottom of this.'

'My sentiments exactly, Chief. My two undercovers and a handful of misfits will be darkening our door any minute now. Should be an interesting night.' Craig gave an exhausted half grin.

'I'm all yours. I told Patti not to wait up,' Riaan said, walking towards the Nespresso machine in his office. 'Short black, yeah?'

'Spot on. Old habits never die.' Craig ran his fingers through his hair, tracing circles along his temples. 'God help us if Gabriella's been murdered. I'm still holding onto that little glimmer of hope that she could just be missing, you know? Had too much of all the attention and is hiding out somewhere, away from the spotlight.'

'Let me make some calls,' Riaan said. 'Get some suits down here. We need as much manpower as possible to get this evil bastard. FBI, CIA. Hell, the NSA, if we must.'

They each took a mug of steaming coffee and clinked them together.

'This prick has messed with us for too long now,' Craig said. 'War has officially been declared. Fuck this piece of shit – his days are numbered.'

Chapter 23

Rip, still reeling from the disappointment of not being able to find his beloved cufflinks, resigned himself to the fact that he must've loaned them to a friend, who, as usual, had never returned them.

'Typical of those schmucks,' he said, as he slammed the basement door and locked it behind him. 'There. All good and clean and fresh. Who would believe what really happened here last night? How exhilarating and completely electrifying. I can't wait for them to discover my beautiful, bold creation, looking positively regal reclining on her chesterfield.'

He couldn't help the giggle that escaped his lips.

'Oh, but my dear Craig will certainly have the hots for me now. Too hot, maybe. I need to get out of town until the dust settles a bit.' He beamed into his bathroom mirror. 'Don't worry, my dear Lieutenant – I won't be gone for long!'

+ + +

On Monday morning, fresh, feisty, and loud, Coco came springing into Craig's office wilder than a three-ring circus.

'Whatcha got there, big fella?' she sang, expecting to hear he'd had a break in the case. However, when he turned around, he looked at her with venom in his eyes.

'Something's happened to Gabriella. She went missing the night before last, and believe me, this ain't a coincidence. I know this fucking psycho has struck again; I feel it in my bones. So, Whoopi, has a print been lifted off that cufflink yet?' His tone became distressed. 'I need answers. Prints. Names. This fuckwit has messed with my brain for too long now. I want his blood – if I have to work around the clock until it happens, then so be it.'

'Today's the day I get results, Lieut,' Coco promptly replied. 'I'll be back in a jiffy, hold thumbs for something positive. See ya shortly.'

As she exited Craig's office, he rubbed his eyes, then called Cody. 'Any news on Gabriella?'

'The teams have split up, Lieut. We're all still searching and unfortunately haven't come up with anything yet.'

'Keep at it,' Craig barked. 'I'm heading down to see the Cantrellos now. I'll touch base later.' He hung up, then lit a cigarette as he drove off.

He made it to the house in record time. Alessandro opened the front door.

'Please tell us you have found my sister, Lieutenant,' he said desperately. 'Please, please, please.'

Craig grimaced and followed him through to the lounge, where Pepe and Francesca sat together on the sofa. He was taken aback on seeing Francesca. She looked gaunt; pain was inscribed all over her face as she sobbed uncontrollably into Pepe's shoulder. The scene was so surreal and unbefitting of the Cantrello household. *I wish I could give her a hug and tell her this was all just some terrible dream,* Craig thought.

'Lieutenant, you find my *bella bambina*, yes?' was all the heartbroken Pepe could release from his lips.

'Nothing yet, Mr Cantrello, but we'll never give up searching,' Craig replied. 'There are numerous teams combing the city as we speak. We *will* find her – make no mistake about that. I'd say sooner rather than later.' He got up and straightened his trousers. 'I need to go home for a quick shower; I've been at the station all night. I'll keep you posted on all developments.'

We're heading towards the critical forty-eight-hour mark, and we all know what that means, he thought. *We need to find her. Fuck!*

+ + +

As the sun set over Champaign, the normally bustling city streets fell eerily silent. The only sounds that could be heard were the faint hum of police radios and the occasional crackle of walkie-talkies. The once-busy commercial district had become a ghost town as every building, both private and public, was meticulously searched. Crowds of officers were gathered at every corner, scanning the area for any sign of Gabriella. Some had binoculars pressed to their eyes, others were walking around with K9 units, but all had one mission: find the city's golden girl.

Skye, the officer heading up the eastern team, approached the Virginia Theatre. She signalled to the team behind her that the front door was locked; luckily, there was a side entrance. Four men and two women entered the building. They ascended the flight of stairs and opened the door, cautiously fanning out and advancing towards the stage. The curtains were drawn.

Skye walked up the stairs and entered through the slight opening of the curtains. What she saw stopped her in her tracks. She immediately pulled the curtain shut and covered her eyes. All she wanted was to block this scene from her mind, but she had to continue. She reluctantly reopened the curtain and stood, staring, her mouth wide open in shock.

The world stopped spinning for that moment – or so it felt. Then, as though a reset button had been pressed, she hollered to the others to immediately come onstage.

Within seconds, the entire team had circled the chesterfield sofa with Gabriella draped over it. The spotlight shone on her pallid skin, the dress and pearls sparkling. With the outfit she was wearing, the damage to her body was hidden. One would say that she was almost elegant. Juliet, in repose.

Instinctively, the other female officer leaned forward to feel her pulse; as she did, one of Gabriella's arms slid down off the arm of the sofa.

'She's gone,' the officer said sadly. Skye immediately called the coroner, then Craig.

Craig didn't even cut the call. He raced down to his car and sped to the theatre. He charged up the stairs, already breathless, identifying the sombre mood on stage straight away. By now, the other teams around town had been alerted. Officers poured into the theatre. Craig promptly called off the search and restored a little law and order at the scene. Tape was placed around the theatre, and forensic detectives set to work.

Barry Blake arrived soon after Craig and officially pronounced Gabriella dead. He ascertained that, apart from the obvious multiple stab wounds, she had defensive wounds on her arms and hands and additional bruising and abrasions that suggested a prolonged struggle with the attacker. Bizarrely, the stab wounds appeared to be the result of at least two different cutting instruments. This monster had made a statement with surgical skill they'd never seen before, dehumanising this angelic girl, stripping her of everything.

'This bastard raped her,' Barry said to Craig. 'He's nothing more than a predator. I hope to God we find some semen.'

Craig took a deep breath, shaking his head, then turned to Barry. 'Make no mistake, this swine is pulling out all the stops, and unfortunately for us, he's a master at covering his tracks. Shit Doc, I hope he did slip up and leave a trace… I guess I can't prolong the agony any longer. I need to notify her family.'

As Craig descended the stairs, Barry let out a shriek. 'He's done it again, Lieutenant! Her left earlobe has been cut off in the same jagged manner as before.'

Craig ran back to the body, examining the ragged skin. Sure enough, it was the same as Leigh.

Barry cleared his throat. 'I know you hate the phrase "serial killer"–'

'*Repeater*,' Craig said. 'But I'm afraid to say this is a repeater with a difference. What we're seeing now is an escalation. He's spinning out of control, no longer able to contain his rage; his obsession is taking over. We undoubtedly have a serial killer on the loose.'

Gaze fixated on the girl he had been unable to rescue, Craig flicked open his lighter and lit a cigarette. He was quick to explain to the officers that it was the stinging fumes of smoke, not tears, that caused his eyes to water.

Chapter 24

Before visiting the Cantrello family to deliver the heartbreaking news, Craig gathered his team at the station for an emergency briefing. 'Time is of the essence, and I need everyone to give their complete attention to this case,' he said. 'Riaan has already deployed a skeleton crew to run the station, and I've been granted full authority to establish a robust task force. As we speak, our chief is coordinating reinforcements from Chicago, Indianapolis, and St Louis to provide additional support for this critical investigation.'

He scanned the room, meeting the eyes of each individual officer as if sizing them up. 'We all know that ten percent of the cops in any PD do ninety percent of the work, right? This intelligence unit is part of that ten percent; that's why you're sitting in this room. I have faith in all of you. Now, with the borrowed brood arriving anytime soon, let's make it happen and catch this monster.' He dismissed them all, instructing Cody to go down to the coroner and get a copy of his report.

Twenty minutes later, Craig arrived at the Cantrello home. You could see something was amiss: it lacked that effervescent Italian hospitality. Adriano answered the door and immediately ushered Craig into the living room. The entire family was already seated, along with Bjorn, who'd arrived on an early-morning flight, waiting in anticipation for any news on Gabriella. Craig rapidly perused the room, locking eyes with Pepe and Francesca.

There was no easy way to tell them the shattering news. *Best to just come straight out with it,* he thought.

'I'm sorry, but–'

He couldn't even finish the sentence before his voice broke. There was an instant, deathly silence, then all hell broke loose. They all jumped to their feet and huddled around Francesca, who remained seated. The room was bursting with raw emotions, tears and wailing; not a single English word filled the air.

This was truly a family united in happiness and sorrow.

'*Il mio bel bambina preso da me in un modo scandaloso,*' Francesca screeched, her voice piercing. '*Non posso accettare questo, non posso prendere il dolore.*' Without another word, she barricaded herself in Pepe's arms, weeping uncontrollably.

'My God, who would do such a despicable thing?' Leonardo shouted, putting his arm around Alessandro.

Franco cleared his throat and said, in a low-octave voice, 'We will stop at nothing to pursue our sister's killer – absolutely nothing.'

Pepe escorted Francesca out of the room. She had fainted once, and with her gasping for breath, he feared she was heading for cardiac arrest. He summoned Adriano, telling him to call the family physician to sedate his devastated mother.

As Craig stood up to leave, he heard Alessandro mumble, 'I will never give up searching for that fucking bastard. He will have me to contend with.'

Chapter 25

The next morning, Kirsten rushed through the station's turnstile doors and headed straight to Craig's office.

'What in God's name is going on, Craig?' she said. 'This is ludicrous, totally senseless. Any leads?' She sat down, dabbing her brow and fixing her hair.

'Nothing yet. My undercovers managed to arrest a few lowlifes for unrelated incidents. In that group is Sebastian Hampton, a person of interest who I'm gonna take to the cleaners in a very short while.' Craig had been deep in thought when Kirsten burst in and was quite irritated by her timing. 'Best make your visit snappy. I'm running late for an emergency meeting with Riaan before I interrogate that scum so, sorry, no time for your usual antics.'

'You're upset about Gabriella. I am too. So, I'm just going to pretend you aren't being a complete asshole.'

'Pretend somewhere else. I have work to do.'

'Oh my God,' she said. 'I've put in a lot of overtime on this as well. You know how invested I am. I've narrowed down a few theories, and I feel there's something here… it's like that case we worked on in Jefferson Park. I was just hoping to jolt your memory and thrash a few suggestions around.'

'Later, Kirsten.' He waved her off. 'I have to go.'

'No,' she said, fuming. 'Not later. I'm done with your disrespect. I'm out. I'm going back to WCIA, where I know my input means something.'

She got up and briskly walked out of his office, her thoughts swirling as her heels clicked on the concrete. *This case is seriously getting to him. I just wish he would let me in like he used to. We've always worked so brilliantly together – why is he shutting me out now?*

Oblivious to what she'd just said, Craig ordered Cody to take Sebastian Hampton to Room Two and leave him there on his own until his meeting with the chief was over. Riaan was quick and precise, enabling Craig to get down to the interrogation rooms without much delay.

Interrogation Room Two was more intimidating than Room Three, based on cop and criminal consensus alike. It was the vibe, most said, the chill that permeated further through you the longer you waited inside. Rumour had it that it was haunted by the ghost of an old captain who refused to leave the precinct, even after his untimely demise. Craig personally suspected it was the slight flickering of a faulty light, barely visible to the untrained eye, playing games with the human mind and dialling up one's nerves. Or, who knew – maybe it was ghosts. These days, Craig was unsure of everything. Might as well add the paranormal to that list.

As Craig entered, he saw a figure huddled at the long table. Although Sebastian appeared to have a calm exterior, the twitch in his eye and the beads of sweat on his forehead told a different story.

Craig closed the door with a bang to test Sebastian's nerves. It worked. Sebastian raised about six inches off his chair.

'Expecting the worst, Mr Hampton?'

'I don't know what to expect, officer,' he said, his voice expressionless.

'It's Lieutenant.'

'I... er, I'm sorry, Lieutenant.' Sebastian seemed to have noticed the visible disdain on Craig's face. 'Why exactly am I here?' he asked, screwing up his eyes and twitchily cracking his knuckles.

Craig pulled another chair out and casually rested his leg on it, ready to launch his attack. He read Sebastian his Miranda rights. With an affirmative answer, Sebastian's rights were waived.

Craig paused, letting the silence seep into the room for a moment, before launching into the interrogation.

'Where were you on Saturday, July 31st, between 12.30 a.m. and 4 a.m.?'

'I'm... not one hundred percent sure, Lieutenant. I think I passed out under the massive oak tree on Branston. That's usually where I end up after a night of binge drinking... which is exactly what I'd been doing.'

'Listen here, *you* clever little dick: I've been around a while, so I know when someone is avoiding a question. Answer me!'

Sebastian's eyes widened. 'I have! I swear – that's exactly what happened.' He seemed to recover, giving a cocky half-smile. 'Do you want me to lie to you, Lieutenant? If you'd like, I can craft some horror story with a bunch of gruesome details to appease you.'

Craig could feel his hackles rise. *What the fuck is this asshole playing at? The audacity of this lowlife... Alright, no more pussyfooting around.*

'Sebastian Hampton,' he said, inching closer to Sebastian's face, enunciating each word. 'Did you murder Gabriella Cantrello?'

'You're right. Take me away!'

Craig stiffened, as if struck in the gut. 'What?'

'You caught me, Lieutenant! Good job. Don't you feel proud of yourself?' He smirked. 'Now, are you done wasting my time?'

'Excuse me?' Craig grabbed Sebastian by the collar of his shirt, pulling him closer until their foreheads were touching. 'Would you like to say that again, Hampton?'

'Well, this is clearly some sick joke, right? Bringing in a bunch of people no one cares about on some trumped-up charges and playing your little detective game? Bet you feel all high and mighty.' Sebastian didn't break eye contact once. 'We both know Gabriella

Cantrello is alive and well. Probably dancing up a storm as we speak.'

Craig was about two seconds from losing it. 'Is she really? And what makes you so sure of that?'

Sebastian snorted. 'Because everyone in the city knows her parents were throwing her a party. I guess my invite got lost in the mail.'

Craig's phone rang, and without a word, he exited the room. Sebastian was left alone once again, this time under the watchful eye of the camera – affectionately known by all the staff as Cameron – mounted on the cracking ceiling. After instructing Cody to monitor Sebastian's moves from the next room, Craig went straight to Riaan's office, kicking the side of the door as he entered.

Riaan just looked at him sympathetically. 'So, what's the verdict? Do we have our possible suspect?'

'He wants to play games with us. I'm leaving him in there for a few hours, on Cody and Cameron's watch. Let him build up a little sweat.'

+ + +

After a substantial amount of time, the door to the interrogation room swung open with noticeable vigour.

'Why the pensive look, Sebastian?' Craig asked, looking straight into Sebastian's bloodshot eyes.

'I've been here for hours,' Sebastian said. 'Apparently, I'm under arrest and still haven't been processed. I demand to call my attorney.'

'Sorry, we can't have that.'

'I won't answer any more questions until I have legal advice. You're not listening to a word I'm saying.'

'I read you your rights,' Craig said. 'You waived your right to a lawyer at present.'

'Whatever bullshit you're trying to pull only applies to murder suspects,' Sebastian said.

So, this minefield of sadness and misunderstanding suddenly has a spark and a little knowledge of the law, Craig thought. *He's obviously been in this predicament before.*

'Oh, well. I hadn't thought of that. It's a good thing, then, that the allegations of murder place you on that suspect list.'

Sebastian's face went even paler. 'You're not gonna get away with this.'

'I'm not *getting away* with anything,' Craig sneered. 'I'm just being thorough by taking these allegations into account,' With that, he slammed the door behind him.

Ten minutes later, he re-entered the room, leaning against the doorframe. 'Pacing. Right on schedule. You do realise that's the first sign of a man who's losing it, don't you?'

'It's called walking,' Sebastian said, pulling at his frayed belt.

'Call it what you want; I know what I'm seeing.'

'Yeah? So do I,' Sebastian replied. 'You have nothing on me. You can't prove anything, least of all that I was at any murder scene.'

'You think I don't have just cause to include you on the list of probable suspects? Well, Mr Hampton, I would be negligent if I didn't investigate a person of interest with ties to our murder victim. Then again, you never know what a thorough background check will turn up.' Craig confidently strode toward the door, exuding determination in each step. Just as he was about to turn the crooked handle, he heard Sebastian speak.

'Wait,' Sebastian said, his voice quiet. 'Is... is she dead? Gabriella?'

'Yes. She is.'

'I didn't kill her,' he said. 'I wouldn't kill her. I loved her.' The last part was barely audible to Craig.

'Sure you did, kid.'

'Go ahead,' Sebastian said, more confidently. 'Do your background checks so I can get out of here. All this is doing is making me bored stiff, and – as I'm sure you've gathered – I'm highly irritable.' He even had the audacity to pout.

'Well, don't fret. I can take care of that for you,' Craig said, slamming the door behind him.

'Have you managed to extract any information from Hampton yet?' Riaan asked, as Craig passed him in the hallway. 'We can't hold him forever.'

'I'm going to break this little ass-wipe soon,' Craig said. 'Just give me a little more time.'

'We need this to work, Craig. Otherwise–'

'I've never let you down before, Chief. Just let me do my thing.' Craig brushed his shoulder past Riaan and continued down the hall. As he made his way back to his office, he dialled Coco's number.

'Whoopster, you got that print? I'm blue from holding my breath, here. And what's happening about the purple fibre and dog hair?'

Without missing a beat, she announced, 'Even under my slew o' paperwork, I'm still on top of it, boss. I was gonna inform ya of the results within the hour.'

'So, what do you have?' Craig bellowed in a high-pitched tone. 'For fuck's sake! I've got a moron in Room Two, two unsolved murders, other suspects running around as we speak, and you tell me you *were* going to notify me of the results within the hour? Jeezus, if I hadn't called you, would that have happened?'

He heard Coco swallow deeply.

'I'm sorry, sir. I shoulda brought ya the results immediately. I'll be there in five.'

Craig felt horrible; he'd never heard Coco sound so dejected. He opened his mouth to apologise, but she hung up before he could get the words out.

Shortly afterwards, she stepped into Craig's office. Immediately, from the way she entered the room to the firm look on her face, he could tell that she'd collected herself and was ready to overlook what had happened and get down to business.

There were a lot of reasons he liked Coco, and that was right up at the top of the list. She didn't let anything stop her from getting the job done.

'No obstacle, no impediment, no challenge is insurmountable,' she said. 'And, finally, I believe we have a break in this case. I forgive you for stealing my thunder under that black cloud outburst you had a few minutes ago.' Craig winced.

'With some fancy tech from the CIA, we've found that the print belongs to a Latin American from the Midwest; we suspect he could be from Kansas. Alison and her team are working in collaboration with the people from Nebraska, Missouri, Oklahoma, and Colorado. The dog hairs found on the rug belong to an Irish setter. Any flags raised?'

Craig exhaled a sigh of relief. 'Fuck me sideways. Finally, we have something! Whoopi, you're a genius! Thank you. And... well, I'm sorry for my behaviour. The stress is starting to get the better of me, I'm afraid.'

'All right,' she said, the grin returning to her face. 'But only 'cause I like ya.'

'Can you please get Alison to prepare a Domain Management file? Then have a look at the database, check on all the Latin Americans living in those areas, and I'll give the suits a call.' With each word, his mood elevated to a new height.

After Coco hurried off to do just that, Craig shrieked, 'Yes!', pumping his fist. 'Fucking amazeballs. And what do you know? An Irish setter. Oh, Mr Hampton, you're about to shit blue bricks.'

He slammed his office door on his way back to the interrogation room. 'Is a pig pork?'

Sebastian glanced up and didn't bother to reply. He bowed his head again, staring at the holes in his weathered sneakers.

Feeling confident about the recent findings, Craig implemented his upper hand and began to taunt him. 'The problem is, Hampton, you're not the reliable authority on what you are saying, have previously been saying, or are going to be saying tomorrow or next week. The only thing that's explicitly obvious is that I have power over you right now. So, brace yourself, Doris; you're in for the ride of your life.'

'You have nothing, dickhead,' Sebastian said, without looking up. 'And I'm still waiting for my attorney. I'm not saying another word until he gets here.'

'My team are on their way to bring in your dog for DNA testing, so make yourself comfortable. You're checking into Hotel CPD for an extended stay.' Craig bared his teeth in a grin. 'And yes, you can make that call now.'

Chapter 26

Rip had settled back into his routine, thriving on all the attention he was inadvertently receiving.

'Word has it that Sebastian's in for questioning.' He shook his head. 'Such a waste... that boy had so much potential, but alas, the drugs and alcohol got the better of him.'

He chuckled, casting his mind back to Sebastian's very first encounter with crack cocaine – it had nearly been his last, when the broken pipe slashed his neck.

'I wonder if he missed that rug,' Rip said, suddenly cold and calculating. 'He sure did get attached to it. Well, that's just another little puzzle piece added to complicate

Sebastian's complex catch-22. Poor thing. He never saw any of it coming. Drugs can addle the brain, after all.'

His laughter echoed against the walls of his basement as he stared at the photo in front of him. He was ready for his next target.

+ + +

On Thursday, with Sebastian in custody, Craig was still awaiting the results of Sebastian and the dog's DNA tests. Sebastian had argued that a familial DNA database search was an invasion of his Fourth Amendment rights, but due to the sensitivity of both cases and the probability of a serial killer being on the loose, his appeal had landed on deaf ears. Craig had just shook his head in amazement.

Meanwhile, Coco and her team were bustling with urgency. The laboratory was teeming with employees labouring beyond their regular shifts. The coroner had gathered specimens from Gabriella's corpse, and like

Craig, was anticipating the results. The prolonged waiting was agonising for Craig.

Craig called Pepe to give the update that the FBI, CIA, and NSA were now involved because of Riaan's enforcement. This was a relief for Pepe, even though it didn't ease the pain of his daughter's passing.

'*Congratulazioni!* You no give up, Lieutenant. *Grazie mille.*'

He went on to say that Francesca had been hospitalised with cardiac complications and that his sons had extended their stays until further notice, eager to assist in any way possible.

+ + +

Rip was busy crafting his next letter. Following up on each masterpiece was a challenge, but one that he was enthusiastic to tackle.

'Have to keep dear old Craig on his toes, don't we? Time to turn his attention back to me. I think this one is gonna work wonders. Should blow a few things out the water, methinks.' He chuckled and started singing.

'Three green bottles hanging on the wall.

Three green bottles

Hanging on the wall

And if one green bottle

Should accidentally fall

There'll be two green bottles

Hanging on the wall

Two green bottles...

One green bottle...

There'll be no green bottles hanging on the wall.

'Oh, dear. What have I done? Three questions for the million-dollar answer: Who, what, where? I'm not schizophrenic. Nor am I!' He laughed irrepressibly. 'This could take quite a while to work out. We're still not on the same wavelength, Craig.' He paused, then emulated the lieutenant's voice. 'Damn, what's wrong with you? Get with the program, boy!'

He cut out the letters and hastily pasted them on a piece of paper, not as neatly as the previous ones.

'Time to get this mailed, or should I leave it somewhere to be discovered at the police station?' He pondered over this for a while and decided to mail it instead. He had other things to do and people to see.

+ + +

'I have to say, this one has got me,' Craig said, staring at the envelope that taunted him. He sat down, elbows on his desk, cradling his head in his hands. 'I'm totally stymied. Wanna give it a shot, Cody?'

'Nah, Lieut, you're the criminal whisperer here,' Cody said, a half-hearted grin on his face. The exhaustion rolling off everyone in the precinct was palpable. 'But you shouldn't stress. You'll work it out – you always do.'

'Yeah,' Craig grumbled. 'How could Sebastian have sent this from custody? Was it even him?'

'He could've scheduled it before we took him in. Maybe he's just trying to throw us off the scent?'

Craig groaned, rubbing his eyes. 'Maybe. Can you give me five, Cody?'

With that, Cody dismissed himself.

'*Sassie Moggie*... that's a reference to someone. Or maybe something?' Craig stood up, stretched his back, and straightened his tie. He walked towards the whiteboard, eyes fixed on the elusive letters. Before interrogating Sebastian, he wanted to figure the note out himself.

The bastard certainly isn't making this easy for me. Let me run through the alphabet and see if I can trigger off anything.

While he was deep in thought, there was a knock on his door. He welcomed Connor into his office. 'This must be telepathy,' he said, delighted.

'Word has it you received more communication from our favourite psycho,' Connor said, stepping in and staring at the whiteboard. His thin eyebrows furrowed. 'Let's get to it, shall we?'

Craig stuck the latest addition on the whiteboard with the rest of the letters. They rehashed the contents, scribbling down various theories.

'No one named Sassie in Champaign, I'm afraid,' Connor said. 'No Moggie either.'

'Could be out-of-towners,' Craig muttered, chewing on the tip of his pen. 'Or perhaps a nickname?'

'Not likely. I don't think they're names.'

'I didn't think so either. I think it's a message.'

They sat there for some time, trying to use every cipher key they had available. The lights at the precinct started to go off, one by one, and the cold cups of coffee that sat on the desk beside them multiplied in number.

'Should we call it a night?' Connor asked, as he stretched against the solid chair. 'My eyes are so tired that everything's swimming.'

Craig froze. He muttered under his breath, then stood up.

'Wait… no. Oh, no.'

'What?' Connor sprang out of his seat.

'It's a code,' Craig said, rubbing his face. 'Look. *S, A, S.*' He pointed to each letter. 'Think about the killer. His victims.'

'Leigh and Gabriella?'

'What did they have in common?' Craig asked. 'What were they known for? They were both famous. Both stars that drew his psychopathic eye.' He pointed to each letter again. 'Swim. Act. And–'

Connor's eyes widened. 'Sing.'

'Could be. Everyone knew those girls came in a trio.' Craig's voice was shaking. He couldn't lose another one. Not on his watch.

'You're saying a third murder is inevitable,' Connor said. 'But wait. Anastasia isn't even in Champaign, and you've got the suspect in holding, haven't you? How do you think he's planning to get to her?'

'I'm not sure, but we're not taking any chances. I'll call the chief now to organise something with law enforcement in London. She needs protection.'

Chapter 27

The next day, Barry Blake called Craig to advise him that results had come through. Craig immediately got into his car and headed downtown to the coroner's office. Entering the lab, he observed the delighted expression on Barry's wrinkled face. He then turned and saw Coco, along with a few of her colleagues, standing beside the gurney.

'So,' Craig said, 'what's up, Doc?'

'You're not going to believe this! The DNA lab came back with a match. The dog hair belongs to Paddy, Sebastian's dog. And, doubly damning, Sebastian's DNA was found on the fibres from the purple rug.'

'At long last!' Craig bellowed. 'We have a fucking breakthrough! I'm gonna nail his lily-white ass to the floor right now.'

They all high-fived and hugged at this incredible news. Craig called Riaan, asking him to contact the highly respected judge, the Hon. Thomas J. Clarkson, to arrange a warrant for Sebastian's arrest. The paperwork was completed in record time.

Craig went down to the holding cells to officially arrest Sebastian for the murder of Leigh O'Rielly and under reasonable suspicion of the murder of Gabriella Cantrello.

'Well, well,' Craig said, entering the cell, waving the warrant through the air. 'What were you saying before? We've got nothing. Well, the Illinois legal system may disagree with you there.'

He slammed the paper down on the table. Sebastian scanned it quickly, his eyes widening.

'I don't care what your DNA results prove!' Sebastian screeched. 'I was nowhere near Leigh at the time of her death and most certainly never had a grievance with her. She was always nice to me. You have the wrong person in custody. Go look for the real killer!'

'Yeah, right, OJ.'

'I want an attorney,' Sebastian said. 'Now.'

'Can you even afford one?' Craig asked. Sebastian looked down and said nothing. 'Yeah. That's what I thought. We'll have a state attorney appointed for you.'

After hours of interrogation, extreme scrutiny, and a polygraph test, Sebastian's physiological responses to the diagnostic questions were found to be greater than those during the relevant questions. This immediately cast some doubt upon his guilt.

'These results don't tie up with all the evidence stacked against him, Craig,' the examiner said, rather perplexed.

'Then what's with his and his hound's DNA on the rug?' Craig asked furiously. 'They were there, which means that little bastard isn't going anywhere. We couldn't get more conclusive evidence if we tried!'

He slammed the door on his way out and stormed back to his office, throwing himself into his seat.

'Who do those prints on that fucking cufflink belong to? I need an answer now!' Craig barked down the phone. His anger went unheard – the call went straight to voicemail.

'Jeezus, those morons are incompetent,' he said, slurring in a blind rage. 'What do they do all fucking day? Sit with their fingers up their asses? It's taking so long, anyone would think there were a billion fucking Latinos in the US!' He shoved himself up and stalked to his whiteboard. 'I'm missing something here, and I bet it's staring me in the fucking face. I just know it.'

The steady clip of heels broke him out of his thoughts. In the doorway stood Kirsten. She simply raised an eyebrow, as if waiting for permission to speak. In all likelihood, she was waiting to see which Craig she would encounter today – her confidante or the unhinged lieutenant.

'Thought you were done with me,' Craig huffed.

'Please. Who else is gonna call you on all your bullshit and man pain, Ryan?' she retorted. 'Besides, I've just received the greatest news! And it looks like you could use a little cheering up.' Her hand cupped his jaw, gently tilting it upwards. He let out a sigh and nodded.

'You and I have front row seats to Anastasia's next concert!' she said.

He crinkled his nose. 'Really? You expect me to pack up and fly to England now?'

'No, of course not. That's the best part! Anastasia's coming back to Champaign!'

'What did you just say?' Craig asked, halfway between confusion and rage.

Kirsten carried on as if she hadn't heard him. 'I've persuaded her to come home before her world tour. Well, more like *asked* – she didn't take a lot of convincing. We were looking for a way to raise awareness of domestic violence and violence against women in general, and I thought it would be perfect!' She clapped her hands together. 'What better way to spread the message than a charity concert? And it would be a great way to boost morale for everyone in Champaign – God knows they need it.'

Craig's nostrils flared. He shoved a hand through his hair.

'What's wrong, Craig?'

'I'm sick of you fucking meddling in police affairs! When will you ever bloody learn to keep your interfering nose out of official business?'

'You can't talk to me like that.' Crossing her arms, Kirsten narrowed her eyes.

'The killer's going after her next! Anastasia's been placed under police protection in London. She's been ordered to stay there until *we* decide it's safe.'

Kirsten sat there, staring at him in utter shock. For once in her life, she was briefly at a complete loss for words. 'I... well... I wasn't aware that travel restrictions had been set. She most certainly didn't mention anything to me. I was in media mode and was trying to do something good for this place.'

Without batting an eyelid, she got up and traipsed out of his office. Craig just shook his head in disbelief.

As Kirsten left, Riaan walked in and closed the door behind him.

'You better sit down for this one,' he said.

'What's up, Chief? Believe me, my day can't possibly get any worse, so throw all you have at me. I'm as ready as I'll ever be.'

'The print on the cufflink,' he said. Craig immediately straightened. 'It belongs to an out-of-state criminal, Ramon Martinez. He was incarcerated at Lansing Correctional Facility in Leavenworth County and released several years ago. He has no known links to Champaign, the girls, or Illinois for that matter.' Riaan grimaced.

'Fuck that,' Craig spat. 'I'm not giving up on that little prick Sebastian with all the evidence we have on him. I don't give a shit if they say it's circumstantial. Come on, boss man. Let's go for a little walk to the holding cells.'

He and Riaan led Sebastian back to the interrogation room in handcuffs. As Sebastian sat down, Craig, without hesitating, threw the cufflink onto the table. Sebastian glanced at it, and his pupils dilated.

Craig knew that look: recognition.

'Missing something?' he asked. 'Looks like you won't be going to any more parties anytime soon.'

There was no fear, no guilt, on Sebastian's face when he responded. Only – infuriatingly – a smirk. 'Nope.'

'It's not yours, then?' Riaan asked.

'Nope,' he repeated. The smile grew wider.

Craig slammed his hand on the table. Sebastian winced. 'Talk. Now.'

'It's not mine,' Sebastian blurted out. 'But I know who it belongs to.'

'Of course you do,' Craig sighed. It was par for the course that this little asshole was trying to worm his way out of it. 'Spill the beans, boy.'

'Not so fast, Lieutenant.' The smirk was back. 'If I'm going to be helpful, I need my attorney present. I'm not uttering another sound until I see him in person.' He leaned back in the broken chair; as he did so, it let out a long creak.

STRIKE 3

Chapter 28

Anastasia had disregarded all instructions, including those of her husband. Sinclair was furious with her. As they were en route to the airport early on Friday morning, he attempted one final effort to dissuade her from proceeding with the concert. A fruitless exercise: absolutely nothing worked. The gravitational pull to Champaign was simply too great to ignore. She persisted with this endeavour in honour of her cherished friends.

I'm doing this for you two, she thought as she boarded the plane at Heathrow after saying goodbye to Sinclair. *We'll always be the three musketeers.*

Anastasia had arranged for Marco to pick her up from the airport so they could begin organising the local activities for the event ahead of time. After their meeting, she planned to surprise her parents with her unexpected visit, then relax with them for the remainder of the day. Tomorrow, she would meet with her agent and team to get everything in order. Once that was done, she'd touch base with Kirsten to finalise the media coverage and advertising.

She hadn't spoken to Kirsten since their initial conversation. There had been two missed calls, and a text reading *'DON'T COME HOME – STAY PUT!'*.

In all truth, Anastasia had been avoiding Kirsten; she was a decent actor, but lying was different. How could she possibly tell Kirsten she was under police protection, when no one was supposed to know? Or *did* Kirsten know? Anastasia had seen the gap to go home for a while and taken it. She knew Kirsten would be livid with her, but there wasn't much she could do about it once Anastasia was in Champaign, was there?

As usual, Anastasia and Marco were excited to see each other, even knocking over her suitcase in their rush to hug in the busy airport terminal.

'Ana! It's been way too long. How have you been? We have so much to catch up on, with all your exciting news about your world tour – and are the rumours of a possible little pop princess true?'

'Wow, Mr Carrera, you haven't paused for breath,' Anastasia said, laughing.

'How many times do I have to ask you to call me Marco?'

'Well,' she said, 'you always put on your teacher voice when you tell me. It makes it difficult.'

'We're friends, aren't we?'

'Of course.'

'And you've been out of school for how long?'

'Don't remind me! I think I found my first grey hair the other day.'

'Impossible,' he said, sweeping a strand of loose hair behind her ear. 'Anyway, that's beside the point. Please call me Marco – I insist.'

'Oh, very well. If you insist.' She looked down at her Cartier watch. 'How about a coffee before you take me back to my parents' place?'

'Exactly what I had in mind!' He smiled, putting a finger to his forehead. 'Great minds think alike.'

He opened the passenger door of his red convertible, giving Anastasia a little bow.

'I have a confession to make,' she said, giggling as she slid into the car. 'I've always wanted to drive in this monster.'

She made herself comfortable, stretching her hands out on the leather seat as Marco got in the driver's side. He started the car, before turning to her.

'Ana, do you mind if we swing by my place on the way to Café Kopi? I was in such a rush to get to the airport on time that I forgot to bring my file with all the event information.'

'Sure thing. I'm in no rush.' Anastasia leaned closer to Marco, cupping her hand to her mouth. 'No one even knows I'm in town yet.'

Marco smiled. 'It'll be our little secret, then.'

They drove at full speed, roof down, wind blowing through their hair. Anastasia grabbed the crimson silk scarf at her feet – Marco's, presumably – and draped it around her neck, watching as it fluttered in the air.

What a perfect cab ride, Anastasia thought. She slipped further down into the seat, relishing in the moment.

When they walked inside Marco's beautiful home, Anastasia couldn't stop complimenting it. 'This is undeniably a design masterpiece, Marco. I'm super impressed. I just love your style!'

'Thank you, Ana. I am a sucker for beautiful things.' He led her to the terrace, which was complete with reclining sun loungers and a fire pit. The magnificent pool area that it overlooked was decked out with its own private Arabian gazebo and hundreds of little twinkling lights.

'Why don't we have coffee here?' Anastasia blurted out. 'We'll create our own eclectic atmosphere. I mean if you don't mind. It's gorgeous out here!'

'I'd be honoured,' he said, and excused himself to make the drinks. Anastasia took the opportunity to take it all in - the sun on her skin, the gentle breeze, the beauty of the clear blue water as it rippled lazily. She sat on a sun lounger and kicked off her shoes, wiggling her toes.

Marco returned with two delicious cappuccinos, complemented by a lavish array of biscotti. Anastasia took a sip and a small bite. 'I'm so excited about this concert, Marco. And the fact that it's in honour of Leigh and Gabriella makes it even more special.'

They chatted for a while, reminiscing. When they started discussing the event, she felt her stomach churn. She tried to readjust herself. Suddenly, the world started to blur around the edges.

'Oh, my goodness,' she said, her fingers gripping onto the wooden side of the lounger. 'I'm sorry, Marco. I'm feeling rather weird… Must've been that burrito I ate on the plane. I knew it didn't taste right.'

'Would you like to lie down for a while? We can discuss the concert when you're feeling up to it – no pressure. Here, let me take you to my guest room. You'll feel more comfortable there.'

'Thank goodness we came here first,' she said, feeling increasingly dreadful. 'Imagine if we were at Café Kopi. Oh, the rumours! People really latch onto the littlest things.'

As she made her way back inside, Marco put his arm around her to steady her. Without warning, her legs collapsed. He promptly picked her up and carried her. They headed down a flight of stairs, towards a medieval door carved into an arched grotto.

Anastasia, by now, was quite delirious. She'd broken into a sweat. Miraculously, she was able to stand unaided when Marco put her down. He pressed a button on the wall. As the heavy wooden door opened, she caught sight of photographs of Leigh, Gabriella, and herself placed proudly on the walls within. The pictures were extremely large, blown up to nearly life size.

'What... are those?' she asked, each word an effort. He didn't answer.

Anastasia fell to the ground. No – that wasn't right. She was pushed. She felt the force of a foot hit her stomach once, twice, five times.

She faintly heard movement near her again, prompting her to desperately move away. On all fours, she edged into the room, towards the photographs. The world was spinning, her muscles seizing.

Am I dreaming? What's going on? What's happening to me?

As she turned around slowly, she saw a blurry vision of someone holding... a baseball bat? It was raised to the ceiling.

Marco?

Desperate thoughts swam around in her head. She frenetically tried to focus.

'Marco?' she said, or maybe just thought. Everything was so loud, and she wasn't sure if she was pleading with him to stop or to save her.

Marco...

He struck, smashing her head with the bat, knocking her to the ground. Struggling with all her might, she managed to grab his arm. He flipped her over and savagely started raping her. She continued to put up a fight, clawing his forearm. Then, in her dazed state, she looked up and saw a bright, shiny object in his hand.

'Knife,' she murmured.

In slow motion, she felt a hefty jab in her side. A burning sensation. She tried to pull the knife away and he slashed her wrist. Her arm fell limply, blood running all over her hand. Marco descended into a symphony of organised killing, stabbing her multiple times, and finally cutting off her left earlobe.

'Who? Marco...' Her voice was almost inaudible.

He stood, his dark eyes scanning the room. They lit up when he saw the red scarf still around her neck. He grabbed it and began to pull it taut.

'All those questions,' he said, enunciating every word. 'Too many *fucking questions!*'

She weakly grabbed at her throat, trying to pry herself free, but to no avail.

'You think you get all the answers just laid at your feet, huh? You wanna hear how I ripped the life out of Leigh? About how Gabriella could scream? And I mean *really* scream.' He closed his eyes, savouring the memory. 'Those Oscar-winning crocodile tears of hers paled in comparison to what she was truly capable of. Such raw emotion! I made her scream for hours until she got it just right. I did always know how to bring out the best in you girls.'

He tightened his grip. Anastasia squeaked out a hoarse breath. 'And what about you, huh? You wanna know what's gonna happen to you, Ana?'

He paused for dramatic effect and leaned in closer. She could still smell coffee on his breath.

'You,' he said, his voice barely a whisper, 'will never sing again. Never *speak* again!' His sudden shout made her wince. 'You little tart.'

The flash of silver was back. She let out a little whimper – the only sound she was capable of.

A loud noise came from upstairs. Marco sat up with a jolt. 'What the hell was that?' he shrieked. 'I gotta get out. There's no one here, so where did that fucking noise come from?' His voice, still ranting, trailed off as he dashed out of the room, leaving Anastasia for dead.

Her phone had fallen to the ground next to where she was lying. She managed to press '*3*' on her speed dial and slightly loosen the fabric around her neck.

'Hello?' Craig's voice echoed in the room. 'Hello? Anastasia? Are you there?'

'...Marco.'

Chapter 29

'Forget your fucking attorney! I need the truth. Then this whole mess will finally be over.' Craig's voice cracked. 'Please, Sebastian. Who does that cufflink belong to?'

The desperation on Craig's face was enough to move Sebastian. He shifted in his seat before meeting the lieutenant's eyes.

'It belongs to the one and only Marco Carrera, the upstanding drama teacher at Brentwood Park High. The darling of all the girls.' He bowed his head and burst into tears. 'He gets me drugs sometimes. I thought he was trying to help. Trying to wean me off it nice and slow. He said he wanted to help me… Fuck. He's the one who gave me that carpet you're all hung up on!'

'Shit,' Craig said, shaking his head uncontrollably. 'Shit, how…'

'Craig,' Riaan put a hand on his shoulder. 'Focus.'

'Right. We need a warrant for Carrera's house, pronto.'

Riaan nodded. 'I'm on it.'

Craig turned back to Sebastian. 'Just sit tight. We'll have you out of here shortly.' With that, he rushed out of the room.

As Kirsten pulled into the car park, she saw Craig running. She signalled to him to get into her car.

'Hop in, big boy. You can fill me in on the way there, wherever we're going.'

'We're going straight to fucking Carrera's house. Don't stop at any traffic lights, you hear me?'

'Which one of us was nominated the most likely to end up in a car chase, Ryan?'

'Point taken.' He strapped himself in and had barely closed the door before Kirsten peeled out of the lot. 'That piece of shit is our killer, Kirsten. Jeezus, talk about a wolf in sheep's clothing. That motherfucker had us all fooled!'

The look on her face was indescribable. 'I knew I'd seen those cufflinks before,' she whispered. 'I knew it. He was wearing them at the school reunion. I was sitting next to him and couldn't help but notice them. The emblem intrigued me.'

'It's not your fault,' he said. 'He deceived us all.'

'Leigh and Gabriella would still be alive, if I'd just...' She trailed off, unable to continue, her voice filled with unshed tears.

'He'll pay for what he's done. I promise.'

His phone rang. Anastasia was calling.

'Hello?' he asked. No one answered. In the background, he heard a sob and a convulsive gasp for air. 'Hello? Anastasia? Are you there?'

'...Marco,' was all she said.

'Marco?' His gut clenched.

'She's supposed to be in London!' Kirsten said, panic setting in.

'Are you at his house? Is he with you now? You need to get out of there!'

There was no reply. Only silence. The ragged breaths had stopped.

'Anastasia!' Craig gasped. 'Go faster, Kirsten!'

'You don't have to tell me twice,' she grunted, pushing her foot further down on the accelerator.

They pulled up at Marco's home unscathed, jumped out of the car, and ran to the front door. Riaan pulled up a moment later, armed with the search warrant.

Craig kicked the door open. Each of them ran in a different direction. Craig headed down the stairs, through an old-fashioned door.

The room was empty, except for a figure prone on the ground. He knew who it was. He dashed towards her, shouting her name.

Anastasia's hair was sprawled across the cold tiled floor like a halo. One hand was on her neck, as if still fighting for air; the other lay sprawled out beside her, soaked in blood. Just like Leigh and Gabriella, her left earlobe had been hacked off. He checked for a pulse.

'Anastasia,' he whispered.

There was nothing. Champaign's little nightingale had already passed away.

Devastated, he shed a tear as he looked down at this beautiful young woman, recalling his many liaisons with her and her two amazing friends, all taken so tragically. This was the final chapter in this horrific saga.

Champaign will never be the same again.

Riaan and Kirsten bolted down the stairs to the basement. Their hearts sank at the sight before them. Anastasia's limp body lay motionless on the ground, bathed in a pool of crimson blood. The once-radiant girl now appeared pale and ghostly, her clothing dishevelled and torn.

Kirsten covered her mouth as she tried to keep her lunch down. It was clear that the killer had savagely torn through Anastasia's flesh, and her mind reeled at the thought of what this poor soul had gone through.

Panic-stricken, Riaan called the station. They waited anxiously. It wasn't long before the sound of sirens blared through the suburban streets, announcing the arrival of the police.

'Sassie Moggie,' Craig croaked.

'What?' Riaan asked.

'The last letter I got. It was in code. I worked it out when Connor was in my office.' Pushing himself to his feet, Craig stepped closer to the portraits on the wall. The eyes of the murdered women seemed to be staring straight into his soul. 'It stands for Swim, Act and Sing. SAS. Bastard probably hurled in the rest to throw us off the trail.'

'And Moggie?'

He thought for a minute and shrugged.

Kirsten piped up. 'The girls each achieved something great in their field. A medal, an Oscar, and a Grammy. MOG.'

Craig couldn't peel his eyes away from the photos. 'Jeezus, have you two seen this shit? How in God's name did this despicable creature fly under the radar? He hoodwinked us all.'

Kirsten and Riaan immediately got up from tending to Anastasia's body. All three stood and stared at the beautifully laid-out portraits of the three women. There were photos from high school, showing the girls with round faces and youthful grins; photos taken from magazines and Facebook; and photos they must've sent to Marco themselves over the years. Right in the middle was the article Kirsten had written announcing the girls' return to Champaign.

Craig stood motionless, gazing at one photograph on the wall. It showed the three young women dressed in graduation robes, beaming with joy and gratitude as they posed with their hero, mentor, and friend. The exact one that had caught his eye on the Cantrellos' mantlepiece.

The picture affected Craig more than any other he'd seen in a long time. Perhaps it was because he'd known the girls. He'd talked to them, heard their stories, and felt their pain. Whatever the reason, the image touched something deep inside him, stirring emotions he thought he'd buried long ago.

'This psychopath had his trifecta lined up from the start. These were no random killings; he orchestrated every single element, right down to his bullshit letters.' His knees felt weak. He leaned against the wall, not wanting to look at the body or the photos for a second longer. 'Shit, man, why did it take me so long to figure it out? It was all right here!'

'But you did,' Kirsten said, putting a hand on his shoulder. 'You've found the killer, Craig. And, like you said, he's going to pay.'

At this point, the property was swimming with law enforcement. Riaan returned to the precinct and dispatched an all-points bulletin to notify every officer and state department of Marco's criminal status.

Craig and Kirsten traversed the house, carefully observing every room. The interior was spotless and adorned with sophisticated decor, every space displaying its individuality. They found just one other closed door and approached it warily. Craig opened it, Glock 22 in hand.

No one in sight – just an extremely tidy study.

Craig made a beeline for the desk and sat on the gargantuan swivel chair, a chill running down his spine as he sank into the abomination's throne.

'The sheer horror of what occurred in this exact location is beyond the grasp of any rational mind,' Craig muttered, his heart sinking as he realised that he'd failed to prevent the girls from falling victim to this nefarious creation under his watch. To add insult to injury, Craig had even come to his defence when Kirsten had voiced her concerns. Marco's sob story, gentle disposition, and undeniable charisma had blinded Craig to the truth. He'd believed he was a more competent officer than that, but Marco had fooled him to the end. His gut had steered him astray.

Marco's computer was in sleep mode. Craig put on his gloves and hit the space key. Without wasting time, he examined the browsing history, which showed that Marco had researched alternative approaches to ending life; data regarding puncture injuries, suffocation, and chloroform usage; critical timeframes for livor mortis and rigor mortis onset; and in-depth analyses of various drugs and hallucinogens. The sound of Craig's systematic keystrokes echoed through the silent room as he delved deeper into the morbid subject matter.

'This has so much incriminating evidence... he didn't think he was gonna get caught.' Craig snorted at the audacity of this man. 'We're gonna nail the bastard to the wall.'

As Kirsten sifted through Marco's desk, she stumbled upon a concealed compartment that held even more damning proof. Tucked away inside was an Arizona driver's license bearing the name Marco Carrera, yet underneath all the clutter, she uncovered another license from Kansas. It belonged to a significantly younger man, whose face she didn't recognise, but his name resonated within her.

'Hey, Craig? What was the name of the guy whose print we found?'

'Ramon Martinez.'

'It's your lucky day,' she said, passing him the licence and a few other papers that had been jammed in the drawer. He examined them carefully.

'The print on the cufflink belongs to Ramon Martinez, while Sebastian confirmed the cufflink belongs to Marco Carrera,' he muttered.

'Could be the same person.'

'We'll need to run a check on that.'

'What's interesting is how much his looks have changed,' Kirsten said. 'This picture has green eyes and the other has brown. He's had a nose job and has different cheekbones and teeth – not to mention the moustache. Imagine going to such lengths to alter your looks!'

'There's only one reason someone would resort to those drastic measures, Kirst,' Craig said, as he stood up to stretch his legs. 'This fucking psycho has something big to hide. And I mean *big*. I do believe we've only just scratched the surface.'

They continued sifting through the drawers and found a photograph of a quaint log cabin – the very same one shown on the computer's screen saver.

Chapter 30

Squinting against the late-afternoon light, Craig hesitated on the Carlyles' doorstep for several minutes before finally pressing the doorbell.

I wonder if they even knew she was home.

This was the third time in as many months that he'd found himself in this area, facing the difficult task of breaking hearts and shattering lives. It hadn't gotten any easier, and he doubted it ever would.

As he waited for the door to open, Craig thought about the other families he'd delivered the same news to. They had all been crushed by the evil actions of this monster. He couldn't help but feel helpless in these moments, knowing that no matter how hard he tried, he couldn't change the outcome. He loved his job with a passion, but this part of it left him stone cold.

Anastasia's mother, Lily Carlyle, had come from humble beginnings, a fact she often tried to hide. But after consuming a few glasses of the finest bubbly money could buy, her facade melted away, revealing a woman who was uncomfortable with her newfound wealth and status. She struggled to be accepted in the posh community they resided in – at the country club and all the glitzy gatherings – but could never quite measure up. With true grit, she forged ahead, ignoring the unwarranted nastiness, embracing her fabulous lifestyle, showing off her designer clothes and expensive jewellery. Even though she had a hard exterior, she was warm and caring.

Brady, Anastasia's father, came from a well-off background and did everything within his power to boost her confidence. He worked to make her feel comfortable and cater to her every whim. Lily's relationship with her daughter was more complex; she was closer to her son, Patrick. Anastasia had always been her daddy's little girl.

Lily opened the door, appearing rather shocked to see Craig. 'Has something happened to Patrick, Lieutenant?'

'No, Mrs Carlyle. I'm afraid it's about your daughter.'

'Do come in,' she said, frowning. Nonetheless, she made way for Craig to enter and showed him to the living room. 'What has Anastasia done? It's not like her to have a brush with the law.'

'Mrs Carlyle, is your husband home?'

'He's at the office.' She bristled. 'You're making me nervous, Lieutenant. What's my daughter done?'

'Mrs Carlyle, please sit down,' he said, and she complied. 'I'm afraid... well, there's no easy way to say this. Anastasia was murdered a short while ago.'

The atmosphere in the room was tense and quiet. Suddenly, Lily broke down in tears and reached for her phone, urgently dialling Brady to deliver the heart-wrenching news.

Craig was still present when Brady arrived, gasping for air, and overcome with grief. Lily embraced her husband.

'Lil,' Brady choked out. They held each other tightly for what seemed like an eternity to Craig before Brady turned his way. 'Do you know who's responsible for killing our beautiful baby girl?'

Craig grimaced. 'Yes. My colleagues are hunting him down as we speak.'

'Who?' Brady hissed.

'Marco Carrera.'

You could have knocked them over with a feather. They both stared at Craig in total disbelief.

'What?' Lily said. 'He loved our Ana!'

Brady flinched. 'I should've known. I never liked that punk. Never. But Ana… she always insisted he was a good man. I'm going to *kill* him!'

Lily went to cup Brady's face. 'Dear–'

He pulled away, screeching. 'He's a fucking monster, Lil! He murdered our baby!' He turned to Craig. 'You gotta nail this bastard. Where is he? Where *is he?*'

Lily held him in her arms as he broke down. They screamed and cried uncontrollably, trembling as they consoled each other. Craig gave them each a hug.

'He'll never see the light of day again,' Craig said, raising his fist and placing it on his heart. 'That's a promise I intend to keep, and that goes to all of you.'

'Where... where is our daughter now, Lieutenant?' Lily asked, barely releasing the words. 'I need to see her. We both need to see her.'

Before Craig could reply, he received a call from Riaan, instructing him to go back to Anastasia's crime scene. He apologised to the Carlyles, assuring them he had everything under control, and they would be able to see Anastasia a little later. Though the words flowed smoothly, there was a faint sense of distance in his tone.

He was used to playing this game. Used to separating himself from his emotions to achieve his goals. He knew that it wasn't healthy, that it wasn't how things should be, but he couldn't help it. The constant push and pull of his desires versus his duties had long since eroded away the softer edges of his soul.

Outside the house, he felt a familiar weight in his hand. Without hesitation, he pulled out a cigarette and lit it. The smoke curled up in the air like a ghost, its tendrils floating off into the atmosphere, unbound and carefree. A stark contrast to the way he felt.

He stood there for a moment longer, staring out into the abyss of his thoughts, before finally nodding his head and making his way down the garden path. The door clicked shut behind him. For a second, he felt something stir inside of him. Something that he couldn't name or understand. But, just as quickly as it had appeared, it was gone, buried once more beneath the facade he had so carefully constructed.

Chapter 31

Marco pulled over onto the shoulder of the interstate to stretch his legs. He climbed over the guardrail, not giving a thought to the danger. He had a long road trip ahead, bound for his cabin across state lines.

'No, *you* fuckwit, it was all your idea,' he hissed. 'Do you realise the magnitude of the drama you've caused? I told you to stop while we had the upper hand. You never fucking listen to me and always go off on a tangent at a million miles an hour, without giving any thought to the repercussions it may have.'

'Dry your eyes, you little curmudgeon!' Rip screamed back. 'We always find our way out of difficult situations, so instead of crying me a river, get a plan of action going! We're sure gonna need one *ahora*, dickhead.'

'Why don't you bitch-slap each other, kiss, and make up?' Surly asked. 'Only then can we figure out something together, without all the theatrics. You need to think rationally, like most women.' He chortled, then the expression on Marco's face changed at the thought of that.

Marco instantly distanced himself from these two personalities. Mentally setting his seat into the reclining position, he went back to the evening of Leigh's murder.

He'd lost count of all the erotic lovemaking sessions they'd had. God, it had been good – maybe he should've kept her alive a little longer. He could've snatched her away from that prick Chad for his own fulfilment at the drop of a hat. She was a true siren, that one; he was getting all horny thinking about their sexual escapades again. That little *chica* had been tangy and oh-so-tasty – very fuckable indeed!

She'd been kissing him all over when he'd told her he wanted to surprise her with something extraordinary. After placing a blindfold over her eyes, he'd picked her up and carried her down to his 'cellar' to show her his prized alcohol collection. She'd been under the impression she could choose a bottle of French champagne. He'd hinted there was a methuselah of Dom Perignon Rose Gold 1996 waiting for her, at a cool forty-nine thousand dollars apiece. The fact that only thirty-five bottles were produced had impressed her. Ah, how she'd sucked in his bullshit. He'd said the vintage rose had the same aroma as her – smokin' hot – and the same taste: strong, radiant, and sharp, with a firm finish. Yeah, just like her. Firm finish, alright. She'd sure liked that.

You demon, Marco, to lure her to the basement, he thought, giggling. *For that, you deserve a pat on the back!* And as they'd descended the stairs, he'd reassured her of their exciting new life together.

He relived the final rape, becoming more aroused as he visualised each rigid stroke penetrating her warm, wet vagina while he'd asphyxiated her. Her resistance had made it more worthwhile to him.

The ultimate gratification had come from the final thirty-five stab wounds, which he'd enacted meticulously and with the utmost precision. He recollected each jab, right down to the jagged cutting of her left earlobe. He'd placed it in a box with the same insignia as his cufflinks – a *heartagram,* representing the blending of opposites such as love and hate and life and death – adding it to the other earlobes inside.

Holding the box, he'd licked his lips and smiled. After going back to finish Leigh off by tightening that treasured red scarf around her neck, he'd bound her body with duct tape, then wrapped her in an old purple rug he'd given to Sebastian and stolen back for this very purpose. He'd placed her body into the trunk of his car, which had been lined with the other half of the rug. A couple of days later, he'd returned the rug under the guise of scoring more drugs for Sebastian. Any evidence found on it would incriminate Sebastian, and that was all Marco had been concerned about: framing that poor, unassuming addict who didn't stand a chance. He'd then driven to the outskirts of the city and dumped her next to the ravine, so it looked like a random killing.

Back home, he'd cleaned up the mess and polished off his finest bottle of champagne. Not Dom this time. He'd been in heaven, totally satisfied with what he'd accomplished. Looking at the photos of his victims, he'd jerked himself off. He'd remembered every gory detail as if the murders had happened moments ago.

That was when he'd seen it. Through the dim light from the window in the corner of the basement, a yellow glow had hovered over Gabriella's photograph. A sign. Gabriella would be the next to go.

The ringing of his cell phone brought Marco out of his thoughts and back to the current day. After finishing the call, he was riding even higher. Submerging himself back in the flow of his favourite memories, he fondly remembered his induction to the highly secretive cabal he'd joined twenty years ago.

Still reeling from the elation of his first murder, he'd taken a long drive to the Laramie Plains Lakes to engage in some shoreline camping in a primitive setting, far from the madding crowd. It had been a cold and dreary night, the kind that sends chills down your spine. Marco and another figure had stood in the woods at a desolate campsite. They hadn't known each other, yet. Both had been drawn to the spot for their own reasons, as if fate had brought them together.

The stocky man with curly blonde hair, very dark, deep-set eyes, and all-black clothes had approached Marco, who'd been wearing a stained flannel shirt and blood-soaked jeans. They'd exchanged a quick glance. The air around them had been heavy with an unspoken understanding. They were of the same breed – cold, calculating, and heartless.

After a few seconds of awkward silence, the stocky one had spoken up. 'I didn't think anyone else would be here. This is my spot.' There had been a tinge of aggression in his voice.

'I'm sorry,' Marco had replied, his voice calm and steady. 'I didn't know it was reserved.'

A few moments had passed as they'd taken in each other's body language. They had both been ready to defend themselves, but it'd become clear that they were better served as allies. Something had passed between them; something Marco couldn't even begin to explain. It had just felt so right, so comfortable.

They'd dappled in some small talk, and as the evening had progressed, so had their conversation. They'd discussed their victims, their methods, and their philosophies on killing. The stocky man – Eddie – was a pro, highly experienced; Marco had been just a mere novice at the time, and very eager to learn the tricks of the trade from him. Each detail that they'd shared had cemented their growing friendship. They were like two pieces of a puzzle, made to fit together.

The cold night had eventually given way to dawn. As they'd parted ways, Eddie had given him the details of a certain meeting place.

In the shadowed corners of a cemetery lurked the entrance to a secretive club known only to those who dared to venture into its world of terror. This club wasn't your typical gathering spot for those with a common interest – no, it was far more sinister than that. It was a place where the most twisted and deranged individuals came together to indulge in dark fantasies.

The moment Marco had entered the club, he'd known it was the place for him. He had finally come home.

The walls were adorned with gruesome images of murder scenes. The smell of death lingered in the air, making even the most seasoned killers, Marco included, take a step back. *No,* he had thought, *I can handle this!*

As he'd made his way deeper into the club, he'd been able to hear whispers of violence and sinister plots. These were the individuals who took pleasure in the act of killing, the ones who revelled in the destruction of human life. *My kind of misfits! Yeah!*

They were an eclectic group, each with their own unique method of murder. There were the meticulous planners who took pride in leaving no trace of their heinous deeds. Then, there were those who killed on impulse, driven by a need to quench their insatiable thirst for blood.

To join the club, you had to prove your worth. It wasn't enough to simply have a taste for murder – you had to prove yourself capable of taking a life without hesitation. The initiation process was brutal. It involved being dropped into a labyrinth of rooms, each containing a victim who needed to be eliminated. It was a test of both skill and fortitude. Of course, Marco had nailed his, earning his special trinkets embossed with the symbol of the club: the *heartagram.*

As a member, he became privy to exclusive events that were only whispered about in the darkest corners of the city. Members shared a twisted bond, bound together by their mutual obsession with death and destruction. They lived in a world apart, in a world where the rules of society didn't apply. In a world of shadow, where the line between reality and fantasy was blurred beyond recognition.

When Marco had arrived in Champaign, the first thing he'd done was join the club located west of Philo. He'd made great friends there, and boy, did he get loads of tips from those pros. They'd taught him the mastery of cutting and slicing, giving him the best surgical skills in the business, elevating him to the next level in his craft. Once he'd perfected the art, he was like the maestro of a grand symphony orchestra, directing his tools with a precision and fluidity that rivalled even the most elegant musicians. And he intended to perform again.

+ + +

As Craig stepped out of his car early on Saturday morning, he was met with a scene straight out of a crime thriller. Marco's home had been transformed by a barrage of evidence response teams. Special agents were combing the house, while forensic canine consultants were sniffing around every crevasse. DNA analysts were busy taking samples and documenting every inch of the house. Quite frankly, there were far too many suits for Craig's liking – and the crime scene processing unit had blocked the driveway, which angered him even further.

He'd known Riaan had gone overboard with his request for help but seeing it firsthand was a whole different experience. As he made his way towards the front door, he had to dodge several people, all trying to carry out their tasks with the utmost urgency. It was chaos.

'Excuse me, can I get through?' Craig said, his voice barely audible over the flurry of activity around him. He pushed past a few more agents, finally making it to the door.

Upon entering the property, Craig's cell phone rang. *Speak of the devil.*

'Went a little hard on the backup, did we?'

Riaan gave a half-hearted chuckle. 'This is out of Champaign's league, Craig. We needed all the help we could get. Are you at the house?'

'Just got here.'

'Well, good news. We got the results back.'

'And?'

'Marco Carrera and Ramon Martinez are indeed one and the same.'

Craig cracked his knuckles. 'So, we're only looking for one monster.' His fingers brushed his gun, the metal gleaming in the dim light of the porch. 'And when we find him, we're going to take him down.'

'Exactly. How do you feel about Phoenix?'

'I could work on my tan,' he deadpanned.

'I need you to pack your bags and head over,' Riaan said firmly. 'I've got teams on the ground, including the Director of the FBI. They're gathering everything they can about Ramon, or Marco, or whatever the fuck his name is. I need you to meet them there.'

'Of course, Chief. Can I get your permission to take Kirsten with me?'

Riaan hesitated. 'Well, she is a former detective... okay. I'll agree to this under extenuating circumstances. Go down to HR and have them book you both on the next flight out. Keep me posted on all developments.'

+   +   +

Just under two hours later, Craig was flabbergasted by all Kirsten's luggage. As they walked to the check-in counters for their flight to O'Hare International in Chicago, where they would connect directly to Phoenix, he shook his head. 'Jeezus, woman, how long are you going for?'

'For as long as is required – and within that time, I shall be sufficiently attired for whatever the occasion. Now, may I suggest you dial back the sarcasm and help me with my bags?'

Craig slept through the entirety of both flights, his head on Kirsten's shoulder. He was exhausted. His body had been on autopilot since the discovery of Leigh's body, and he'd barely slept a wink in months. It helped, of course, that Kirsten had slipped some of her sleeping pills into his water; a habit from the old days, when Craig had stayed on the scent of crimes until he'd almost dropped dead of exhaustion.

On arrival in Phoenix, they were met by the Executive Assistant Chief of the Phoenix PD, Douglas Ballantyne, who took them straight down to HQ. Craig briefed them on the case, highlighting recent events. When the slide of the cabin appeared on the screen, one of the young officers gasped.

'I'm ninety percent sure that cabin is in Tin Cup, Colorado.'

'Are you certain, officer?' Ballantyne asked.

'My grandparents had a cabin in that area years ago. I'm convinced I've seen it before.' He stepped forward to take a closer look. 'Yes. I'd bet my bottom dollar on it.'

Chapter 32

The FBI profilers had worked tirelessly with police departments across the country to gather information on Ramon Martinez, the killer who'd eluded authorities for so long, and Craig was eager to hear what they'd learned. But first, they had to hear stories from staff at the Lansing Correctional Facility. As they listened intently, Craig and Kirsten heard stories of a charismatic man who could be both kind and manipulative.

Later that afternoon, they boarded a plane to Denver. The Director of the FBI had insisted on compiling a complete profile of the killer, and they were anxious to see what it contained.

In the boardroom of the Denver PD, they were greeted by Deputy Chief Louis Webber, who wasted no time in getting down to business. He showed them and his team video footage of Martinez being interviewed by correctional personnel, and Craig was struck by the man's calm demeanour. But it was when Martinez spoke that Craig felt a jolt of recognition. The cadence of his speech, the tone of his voice... it was all too familiar. Suddenly, Craig knew exactly who they were dealing with.

As he relayed his suspicions to the team, Kirsten nodded in agreement. They had their man, and now they just had to find him before he struck again.

'What is the most valuable lesson you learned during your time in prison, Mr Martinez?' the interviewer asked.

'Well, sir,' Marco – Ramon? – said. 'I would say that I'm a completely different man.'

'Can you be more specific?'

'I don't like who Ramon Martinez is. I never have. I want to be better – I know I *can* be better.' Ramon placed his hands on the metal table before him. 'The most important thing I learned while incarcerated was myself. I learned my triggers, habits, and fears. I learned to view my thoughts and feelings as perceptions rather than undeniable truths. I learned to conquer my emotions, instead of allowing my emotions to conquer me. Hell, I'm even practicing meditation and relaxation techniques.'

He leaned forward in the stark grey chair, expression earnest. 'Sir, I want to remain outside the walls that imprisoned me. I walked through hell. I learned what true powerlessness feels like, and don't want to venture there again.'

'Well, that's good to hear. You have indeed cleaned up your act and been on your best behaviour, but can you tell us why you deserve parole?'

Ramon ran his fingers through his long, dark hair, clearly choosing his next words with care.

'I want to put this all behind me,' he said, putting on a soft smile and staring straight into the camera. 'I am not a bad person. I have done bad things, yes, but I've atoned for these sins.' He clasped the silver cross worn prominently around his neck.

'I want to move on, sir.' His voice began to tremble. 'I want to break free of this cycle of violence. I can't do that if I'm stuck inside a cage. Will you help me, please?'

The tape abruptly ended, the black screen reflecting Craig's furrowed eyebrows and the dark circles under his eyes.

God, I need to sleep.

Craig turned to the deputy chief. 'Yeah, I'm not buying that bullshit. We need to get to the real Ramon Martinez.'

'Here's everything we got on him so far,' Louis said, passing the file over to Craig.

Craig flipped it open and began to read.

Ramon Martinez hailed from Dodge City in Kansas. His father was domineering and abusive, never giving him the time of day. According to the accounts of Dodge City police, who'd often been called in to mediate his parents' domestic violence, when it suited his mother, she displayed a softer side and comforted him. However, she cowered before his father. She would blame Ramon for things he didn't do to halve her own punishment, and he clearly harboured resentment towards her for subjecting him to so much brutality. The FBI believed this could've been an early cause of his hatred towards women.

A lapsed Catholic, Ramon loathed anything religious, including his parents' choice of educational facilities. He was the proverbial ecclesiastical curse of excommunication. Catholicism was drummed into him as a child; however, despite his position as an altar boy, it was clear he'd never wanted any part in it. Reports from the rector of the Cathedral of Our Lady of Guadalupe stated that he was a 'sinful boy', disobedient and quite antagonistic. He would disrupt the other children during service and blaspheme by asking about demonic rituals.

He had a very high IQ and always achieved top honours in his classes at Sacred Heart Cathedral School. His college years were spent at Newman University in Wichita, where he studied a Bachelor of Arts in English with a minor in Theatre. He had been rejected from Juilliard, Yale, the American Conservatory Theater and UCLA. Unable to receive scholarships to any of his other choices, and with no other options, he must've reluctantly accepted his mother's offer to pay for the Catholic university.

Girls never showed an interest in Ramon, until Ava Larsson, a beautiful postgraduate, noticed him. Friends and acquaintances of the couple – mostly Ava's – said the two were inseparable. Ramon was completely infatuated with her, and she with him. They did everything together. There were records of several trips to LA, Miami, Maui. Clearly, they were beach people, chasing paradise. They were young and in love, ready to take on the world.

It didn't last long, of course; the two soon started to argue. Both were strong-willed, stubborn. Both had a temper. Six months later, the unthinkable happened.

'Now, no one knows exactly what incident set Mr Martinez off,' Louis said. 'Ava herself claimed she couldn't remember what they were arguing about – but one day, he just lost it. Ava was found mutilated in her Wichita apartment. She said he attacked her.'

'Damn. Same MO?' Craig asked.

'Surprisingly, no. For one, she survived. Her left ear was untouched. And the technique? Too precise. It was made to appear rage-induced, but I would say each of those stab wounds was meticulously planned.'

'Interesting.'

'Our behavioural experts have determined it's extremely likely the crime was committed by Ava herself. Ramon's trial testimony supported this. He said he left the apartment to cool off and went to a bar down the road. That's where he was picked up by the cops.'

'A match made in heaven,' Craig muttered. 'Guess like does attract like.' He turned back to the file.

The day after the supposed attack, Ramon was arrested and placed into custody. Ava's testimony was so convincing that he was convicted of grievous bodily harm and sentenced to five years imprisonment. He was transferred to Lansing Correctional Facility in Leavenworth County. While in prison, he built himself up physically, likely preparing for his revenge. Not only was he going to destroy Ava, but he would also eliminate every beautiful girl he could lay his hands on. His hatred for women had ultimately manifested.

He kept quiet. Lay low. On the outside, he was compliant, and he attracted very little attention. Because of this, he only served two years and seven months of his sentence and was released for good behaviour.

His physique had changed, which meant his overall appearance required altering. He had plastic surgery and invested in coloured contact lenses. He cut his hair and grew a moustache. The only missing piece of this fresh start was a new name.

Ramon Martinez had died in prison, and Marco Carrera, just like the phoenix, rose from the ashes.

'Right,' Louis said, once Kirsten had perused the file. 'You're all up to speed so, let's go get him!'

Craig stood up and cleared his throat, studying each member of Louis's team. 'I would like to thank you all for going the extra mile and so diligently getting all this information in such limited time – what a sterling effort! This will help us enormously with our investigation. I always believed we were dealing with a psychopath, but quite honestly, he's worse than we expected.'

Craig and Kirsten left for Tin Cup early the following morning in a police chopper, accompanied by members of the SWAT team and Ian, the sergeant who'd recognised the cabin. Back-up officers from the Denver PD and special agents from the FBI were on a second chopper that followed behind. Craig was armed with GPS coordinates he and Kirsten had found scrawled across the map in Marco's basement.

'I'm coming for you, bastard,' he hissed.

Chapter 33

The old mining town of Tin Cup, Colorado, was breathtaking. The sky was a canvas of purple and pink hues as the sun rose above the horizon. All was quiet and still, except for the occasional hoot of an owl or rustle of the wind.

A perfect hideout for a criminal, Craig thought.

The two choppers swooped down towards the cabin, with further back-up in a convoy of eight vehicles. On touchdown, a small army of law enforcement officers, including the heavily armed SWAT team, moved in. Silent and synchronised, they surrounded the cabin. No warning. No explanation. They were there to overcome and subdue, no matter what.

As Craig surveyed the cabin, his heart pounded. A search warrant was tucked into his shirt, and his Glock 22 was ready. He knew the killer was in there, somewhere, waiting to strike. But there was no sign of life.

Suddenly, Craig heard a rustling from within the cabin. Without hesitation, he signalled for his team to move in, spearheading the operation himself.

He kicked the front door in. Seconds later, the cabin was swamped with law enforcement. It didn't take them long to search the interior. There was no sign of anyone. Ian ran to the old wood stove and felt it; it was still warm.

'He's not far,' he shouted.

Craig surveyed the room. The large muddy footprints on the woollen rug seemed innocuous enough, but the trapdoor beneath it told a different story. He swiftly signalled to his team of SWAT agents, and they sprang into action.

One agent deftly slid the trapdoor to the right and threw two stun grenades inside. The sound was deafening. But even in the chaos, Craig kept his head, barking orders to his team as they descended the staircase like a black caterpillar.

Below, Craig and his team came face to face with their target, a masked, shirtless man in crotchless pants with a riding crop. But Craig wasn't fazed. He knew that he had to act quickly and decisively. With a running dive, he tackled the man to the ground, efficiently trapping him with an arm lock. As the man struggled beneath him, Craig pulled off the mask to reveal the identity of their target – Marco Carrera.

There was no doubt about it; this was the murderer they'd been chasing for months. With a fierce determination, Craig held Marco down, refusing to let him get away.

'My, my, who do we have here?' Craig said. 'Never known you to be so quiet. Got anything of relevance to say now, mugshot?'

Marco just sneered back.

'I almost forgot. We have the conundrum queen here, don't we? So, before I bid you bon voyage, listen up.' Craig cleared his throat.

'Orange is the new black,
No red carpet or plaque,
The judge will bring down the hammer,
So, it's off to the slammer,
For you, boy, there's no turning back!'

While Craig cuffed Marco, he saw the monster behind the mask. Marco kicked, cursed, and gave him a look of repulsion; within that look, Craig caught a glimpse of the hatred and evil oozing out of him.

An eerie silence fell. From the back of the room, a faint noise was heard. Ian ran over and found a young girl.

Cowering and trembling, she was hiding behind a curtain, tied to chains suspended from the ceiling, clutching a flog of some kind. She was dressed for the occasion in a cleavage-highlighting corset, fishnet stockings and a black restraining collar. Her eyes were huge, her breathing shallow, her face all drained and pale. She was barely conscious.

'We need a medic!' Ian shouted. With the help of a few more SWAT agents, they released her.

She had noticeable stab wounds, as well as severe bruising, multiple lacerations, and a deep gash to her head. She collapsed in Ian's arms before she could give her name.

Paramedics were dispatched to the scene. Craig handed Marco over to Deputy Chief Louis, who duly escorted him to the chopper. He was detained under the watchful eyes of four agents and the pilot.

Craig and Kirsten stood bewildered, staring at the basement wall. They had never seen anything quite so horrific. Upon the wall was a massive collage with pictures of at least ten different girls. Under each enlarged photo was a name, a home state, newspaper articles of her disappearance, and masses of writing. But the most horrendous part of this room was the contents displayed on an old dresser below the collage.

In plain view, in pride of place, were items belonging to all Marco's victims. He had taken something personal from each girl he'd murdered and set it under her photograph. Some of the trophies were body parts; others were items of clothing.

They stood there, sickened to the core, trying to read the haphazard scrawls and absorb the information under the pictures. If these walls could talk...

As they drew closer to the end of the collage, there were three enlarged photographs of Leigh, Gabriella, and Anastasia. What repulsed Craig even more were the scribbles across the wall underneath Champaign's three champions, in what he hoped was red paint.

Only a matter of time

'Why?' was all he could say, shaking his head in disgust.

The rest of the teams were bagging every imaginable piece of evidence. By the time they finished, there was virtually nothing left in the basement.

Kirsten pulled the curtain aside. She stopped, her entire body ice cold. Six heavy-duty black industrial chains were suspended from the ceiling. They were well-worn and rusty. On closer examination, she noticed blood spatters on the straps and chunks of hair stuck in a few of the links. She turned around, swallowing back the desire to throw up, and looked straight into a glass cupboard filled with handcuffs, straps, masks, blindfolds, whips, and other paraphernalia relating to sadomasochistic fantasies.

Craig grimaced. 'As if we didn't have enough, we've now got a Class Four sexual sadist on our hands as well. Jeezus, what next?'

Upstairs, in a very old, large trunk, they found a cache of guns and other weapons.

'He sure meant business here,' Craig said. 'I wonder how many more surprises are in store for us. Our girls were stabbed, not shot!'

The cache too was seized. Two officers, white in the face, made their way to the front door, desperate for fresh air. They needed to get out of this dysfunction junction. The stench of death infiltrated the cabin, and an eerie vibe pervaded the very walls.

Now, the once-peaceful surroundings were filled with a flurry of activity, as excavators tore up the earth and forensic teams scoured every inch of the property. The sound of the machines echoed through the hills, bouncing off the trees. One couldn't help but wonder what kind of secrets the ground held and what had led to this sudden invasion.

The excavators dug deeper and deeper into the earth as the sun set over the hills. This site, which once held so much beauty, had become a symbol of tragedy and despair. It was a reminder that even the most idyllic places could be shattered by the actions of monsters.

But maybe, just maybe, this excavation would lead to answers.

Chapter 34

On Monday afternoon, Craig and Kirsten flew back to Champaign, handcuffed to Marco as his official police escorts. There was no communication between them on the flight, though not for want of trying from Marco. After touchdown, they drove straight to Champaign PD and were immediately ushered into Interrogation Room Two, where they were met by Marco's attorney, Mr Sean Wild. No pleasantries were exchanged. Craig gave them fifteen minutes in private.

Marco had already been through the booking process. His fingerprints and mugshot had been taken in Denver, but Craig had pushed for the interview to be held in his jurisdiction due to the three most recent murders being committed in Champaign. He'd fought hard; there was no way in hell he was going to let the Feds, or some other precinct, take charge now. He needed to see this through for the girls.

Craig had just received word that a mass grave containing no less than six bodies had been discovered near the cabin, at the rear of the property. The remains had been sent for urgent DNA testing. Sadly, the detective who discovered the bodies would need to undergo counselling due to the trauma of the finding.

Jeezus, Craig thought. *This creature is truly despicable.* It was time to get to the bottom of all this evil and get that sick, feral fuck locked away. Craig would ensure he got nothing less than the death penalty – preferably the gas chamber. First prize would be to have the trial here in Champaign. Failing that, either Wyoming, where the first murder was committed, or Colorado. The Alcatraz of the Rockies would be a good home for Marco.

That level of danger was just what the doctor ordered for that deranged fuck.

Yeah, a super max prison was exactly what he needed. They wouldn't take any shit from assholes who'd raped and killed innocent young women.

No place to hide there, Marco boy. Craig sneered at the graphic vision playing out in his mind.

No. He couldn't afford to let his emotions get in the way. Not now. Not when they were so close. He couldn't make a mistake – he had to remain calm.

Craig took a deep breath, suppressing all the thoughts of what he'd like to do to the monster in the next room, and opened the door.

The mood inside was rather solemn. Sean and Marco were speaking quietly but stopped the moment they saw him.

Craig had obtained permission to utilise forthcoming court exhibits. He was armed with crime scene photographs and reports and counting on this to work in his favour.

'Right, now all the formalities are over, it's time we had a little chat, Marco Carrera – or is it, Ramon Martinez?'

'You are to refer to my client as Marco Carrera,' Sean interjected. 'That is his official name, according to the documents in front of you.'

'Very well, Counsellor.' Craig looked at Marco and couldn't contain himself any longer. 'What did you do to all these girls?' he shouted, waving his stack of photos violently in front of Marco's face.

'The assumptions behind that question are so misguided,' Marco replied with a grin. 'It frightens me.'

Craig took a deep breath and sat down. He needed to revert to his initial plan. So, with a stoic demeanour, he proceeded.

'Well, let me ask you this. We know you were involved in one way or another with all the victims. So, how about you describe for us exactly how this elimination of women started?'

'I don't recall the exact date,' Marco replied, turning his head, and placing his chin closer to his chest.

Hmm. This little bastard is lying already, and we've only just begun.

'Let me rephrase. Where did the first murder take place?'

'I don't know what you're referring to.'

Sean immediately turned to his client. 'You do not have to answer this question.'

'No, it's alright,' Marco replied, then looked up at Craig. 'You were saying?'

'Let me refresh your memory. If we follow the police timeline of all the girls' disappearances, we're looking at June 10th, 1990. That was the day that one Ava Larsson was reported missing.'

At the mere mention of her name, Marco flinched. Craig suppressed a grin.

I've got you now, bastard.

'So, tell me about Ava,' Craig said, moving his chair slightly closer.

Marco looked at Sean, who gave him a slight nod. 'It was June 3rd. I'd done all my research in prison and knew exactly where to find her. She had moved from Dodge City to Cheyenne to allegedly start a new life. Did she honestly think that I wouldn't seek revenge for what she put me through?'

'What *did* she put you through, exactly?'

'I sat in jail for a crime I didn't commit because of that whore. She wasn't going to get away with it – I'd make sure of that. So, when all was said and done, the day had finally dawned for me to strike. I hired a car using my new name and drove up to Cheyenne from Phoenix. I stalked her for a week with no concerns that she'd recognise me; my appearance had drastically changed. She was in a relationship with a local businessman and seemed very content with her life. The look of her repulsed me, so I didn't want to prolong the inevitable.'

A faint smile appeared on Marco's face.

'It was pouring with rain that day. I parked in an alleyway outside her office block. While I walked towards the building, on cue, she came out of the main entrance. I stopped to ask her directions. She was a little aloof at first, but as we progressed, she became more tolerant, as I was acting ignorant about the city. I glanced around and noticed there weren't any people in the vicinity. I knew it was then or never. Pulling out a knife, I pressed it into her stomach, instructing her to walk with me to my car. Absolute terror covered her face. Her eyes were wide... she didn't even blink.'

Clearly relishing the memory, he sighed. 'I demanded she hand over her phone before we got into the car. We drove straight to the crummy motel I'd rented. After we entered the room, I made her strip, then tied her hands behind her back and stuffed her panties into her mouth, sealing it with duct tape. I picked her up and threw her onto the bed.'

He let out a small giggle. 'Can you believe she still didn't know who I was? She was acting all terrified. I mean, really. I've seen her at her best and, believe me, she ain't all sweet and innocent. Nothing scares that one. So, I got closer to her face and stared into her eyes, my saliva droplets framing her dial.' He leaned across the table. 'And then I whispered, *Hell hath no fury like Ramon scorned*.' This time, he burst fully into laughter. 'Get it?'

He waited, but neither of the men in the room spoke a word. His grin slipped off his face.

'I'm unappreciated in my time, truly. And speaking of time, well, I knew I needed to get on with the show. She became my rag doll, my own sexual toy, and nobody was going to stop me. This little vixen would do everything I wanted her to, without any ridiculous excuses. If I heard it once, I heard it a thousand times: *No, Ramon, I don't know if I can do that. I'm too shy to do that. No, Ramon, you want me to do whaaaat?* The *Kama Sutra* became my power play. I only untied her hands when a position required that she used them.'

As Marco was talking, Craig and Sean did not utter a sound. Craig, who was barely even breathing, witnessed how he took delight in reliving that scene, venom rolling off his tongue.

'While in the middle with the pair of tongs,' Marco continued, 'her arm kept collapsing. This infuriated me to no end. That's when I made the decision that every time a woman does something I'm not happy with, I'll stab her. It's my way of cutting out bad habits. As I went along, getting into the rhythm of stabbing, I noticed the angles I entered became less controlled. This issued a better result to leave her badly maimed for life.'

He shook his head. 'There I go again, always steering off topic. It's just that I love talking about it, and never have the luxury of anyone who'll listen. Where was I? Oh, yes, Ava… It was her apt display of hissing and muffled murmurs, along with the perfect execution of the tigress move, that propelled me to another level of humiliation. I screamed at her to roar as if she were communicating with far-off tigers.' He snickered. 'She obviously couldn't do it, seeing as she was gagged, which sent me into a downward spiral. By this time, I'd had enough of her and her whining resistance, so I finished her off, there and then.'

'You killed Ms Larsson?' Craig asked.

Marco's face contorted with rage. 'Don't interrupt! Anyways, before I was so rudely cut off… Yes. That's when I grabbed her red silk scarf and strangled her, then stabbed her what felt like a million times. My rationale was one stab for every month served, but with the frenzy I found myself in, I ignored that and couldn't stop. Words can't describe my hatred for this woman, Craig; believe me, it's not infinitesimal. I pulled out my Smith and Wesson and shot her once in the forehead and once in the heart, making sure she was dead. I stood over her and reminded her that she once broke *my* heart – it was time for me to return the favour. I shot her again in the centre of the body. Then, looking down at that lifeless tart, I decided to cut off her left earlobe, so she could never whisper another lie into anyone's ear again. I love doing that. The more jagged I cut, the better, as I free us from our collective misery.'

Craig took a sip of water. There was no way he was showing any form of emotion in this monster's presence. 'Alright. You wanted to hurt Ava. What exactly was the motive behind all the other killings, then?'

'After Ava's departure, I decided the world would be a better place if I got rid of beautiful women, as they're no use to mankind,' Marco declared. 'They excessively admire themselves and their appearances; they are repulsive, narcissistic, nasty pieces of work, and they thrive on making men like me feel inferior. It's all about the looks to them. If you're not a jock, you're out. That's why I had plastic surgery to achieve my goal. And it worked – look at all the girls who threw themselves at me just because I was the closest pretty face.'

'So, you weren't interested in a specific type when selecting a victim?'

'No, not at all. As long as she was beautiful, I needed to re-carve her face and body so no other man would ever look at her again.'

'In your own words, tell me how you felt when you first realised, you'd killed Ava,' Craig said.

'I experienced an overwhelming feeling of relief. For way too long, I'd been consumed with pent-up anger; it needed to be released. I felt empowered and somewhat liberated.' Then, out of the blue, Marco pitched his voice an octave higher than normal and started blurting out more words. 'Before I chopped her into pieces to fit in my duffel bag, I decided to screw her just once more, for old times' sake. She obviously didn't resist, so I exerted all my power onto and into her.' He looked right into Craig's eyes with a wide, satisfied grin.

What the fuck? We now also have a fucking necrophiliac on our hands? Jesus Christ, this just gets worse as we go along.

'Did you fantasise about what you would do to your victims before, during and after you killed them?'

'Of course I did. What, do you think these were spur-of-the-moment decisions? Every detail was bloody well-orchestrated, and they all played out to perfection. Naturally, I did this with Rip and Surly's help.'

'Mr Carrera,' Sean said, 'you may have waived your rights, but if there are other people involved–'

'No, no... Rip and Surly are my alter-egos.'

Noting the panic in Sean's eyes, Craig stood from his chair. 'Would you like a moment to speak with your client, Mr Wild?'

'If you don't mind.'

Craig excused himself, pulling the solid door shut behind him. He walked to the next room. There, Kirsten, Riaan, and Skye had been watching the interview. He saw the looks on their faces and simply shrugged.

'I left that evil piece of crap to do the talking. It was evident he wanted centre stage for his performance of a lifetime. I've never dealt with such a narcissistic fucker in my entire career.' Suddenly, Craig slammed his fist down on the table, making everyone flinch. 'Mark my words,' he growled, 'we'll bring this monster to justice. We only have information on Ava and look how he's incriminated himself. This is a slam-dunk, Chief. He's obviously defied all advice from his attorney and is enjoying every moment in the spotlight. Would you like to accompany me for the rest of the show?'

'I'd prefer to watch from the sidelines,' Riaan said, nodding towards the two men still in the interrogation room. Frustration rolled off Sean. Marco stared straight ahead, obviously not listening to a word he was saying.

Craig sauntered back into the room and cleared this throat. Both men turned to look at him. 'Right. So, we've heard everything about Ava, but how did you gain access to your next victim?'

'Oh, that was easy,' Marco replied casually. 'I was on such a high from Ava's death, but I realised I needed to get out of town fast. After a small... detour, I headed to

Billings, Montana. On the way, I picked up a hitchhiker, Mia Hunter. I sent her to her maker but kept her body. It was like *Dinner for One*: same procedure. I then continued my road trip to Twin Falls, Idaho. That's where I picked up the charming Harper Galburche.'

As Marco recalled the names and places, Craig picked up the photographs of the girls from his collage, placing them in order of his recollections.

'She put up a nasty fight, that one. Probably bore the brunt of my rage, more so than the others.' He continued without pausing for breath. 'A day later, I drove down to Salt Lake City to look for a nice little Mormon girl. I found the perfect one: Summer Baker. She was eager to get to know me, and I was equally happy to get to know her. I was with her for a few weeks, teaching her all the ropes of S and M, and boy, did she enjoy it. Now there was a classic case of *still waters run deep*. That's probably why I kept her for longer than the others. My desire overtook my obsession. I got such a thrill from educating her – I am a teacher, after all. We fucked and fucked until we had it down to an art form. Perfection.'

He sighed. 'But as it must be in life, that good thing came to an end. Poor Summer met her death just like the others. The only difference was that right until the very end, she still thought it was a game. How the naivety of a young mind eliminates fear when need be!'

After speaking calmly for the past few minutes, Marco suddenly roared: 'But I couldn't help myself! Her innocence was too tempting.' The loud sound echoed throughout the room, making the two other men jump in their seats. Marco's eyes flickered with satisfaction before he returned to his stoic façade.

'I now had four ears in my special little box. Surly kept asking me, *Did you ear that, Marco?* whenever he addressed me, and would shriek for ages. Funny guy, that one. Next, I took a slow drive across to Carson City, Nevada. That's where I met Holly Welsh. She was very intelligent and, like me, enjoyed the finer things in life. We behaved like a couple for a few weeks. We dined and danced, loved, and laughed – the whole shebang. We conversed on a higher level than the others. Then, unfortunately for her, she started challenging me. She thought she was better than me! Ha! I saw through all her tricks and got the better of *her*.'

Marco chuckled to himself.

'It was time to hit the road again,' he said. 'Portland attracted my attention. There, I found the sweet, innocent Grace Rose Evans. That's where I developed my fetish for schoolgirls. The young are easier to lure in, more accommodating. They don't contest everything and do as they're told. So ripe and gullible: the perfect ingredients.'

As Marco continued his dastardly monologue, Craig was finding it increasingly difficult to conceal his disgust. He dug his nails into his knees, willing himself to remain impassive.

'I'd had a very successful stint, with a one hundred percent hit rate. While the going was good, I decided to take a break for a bit, not wanting to raise any alarm bells. My thirst had been quenched for the time being. I'd spanned seven states and six women. It was time to move on, so I took a slow, relaxed drive down to my cabin to bury the bodies. I figured the most decent thing would be to bury them all together, so they could commiserate with one another about the *big, bad, evil Marco.*'

Marco spread his arms like a showman, then rolled his eyes.

'A few days later, I flew from Denver to Champaign. I chose this place as it's a small enough city, easy to blend in to, without much pomp and ceremony going on. Well, there wasn't *supposed* to be, anyway. It was a great place to hide. Brentwood Park advertised for a drama teacher, so I applied and was successful. My acting boots kicked in, and with my warm charisma, I gained the trust of all the students, especially my girls.'

This time, Craig couldn't hide his flinch. Marco laughed.

'Oh, yes. They fast became my favourite students. I built up their spirits, reminding them of their potential. They idolised me and did everything in their power to impress me. What a shame; honestly, I was sad when I realised what I'd created. I knew it was my responsibility to eliminate them all.'

He took a deep breath and looked Craig straight in the eye. 'You see, Craig—'

'Lieutenant.'

'Nah. You're Craig to me now. My goal was for their adoration to blossom in my bedroom. They were all drowned in gold, so I decided they needed to drop down a notch and end on silver. Do you know what I mean?'

'Enlighten me,' Craig said, his jaw tight.

'They would all fall on my sword, so to speak. I would stab each one with my stiletto – one of the most prized pieces in my collection, a fantastic little thing from the Italian Renaissance. I thought it quite fitting. You see, the stiletto is a dagger with a long, slender blade and needle-like point... much like the girls, with their long, slender legs, their elegant stilettos, their sharp minds.' He leaned forward, his eyes glittering. 'A beautiful end for such beautiful creatures.'

Chapter 35

Marco's actions sickened Craig to his core. All he could think of now – apart from the other six poor young women – was the three girls he'd known so well. How could he ever let their families know the extent of this monster's malicious actions, of the trauma he'd bestowed upon those lovely souls?

Anastasia. Gabriella. Leigh...

My poor Leigh. I'm so sorry.

Craig walked out of the room. Their murders were playing over and over in his mind. He needed a breather.

'Oh dear, have I said anything to offend him?' Rip questioned, observing Craig's exit.

Sean opened his mouth, but before he could speak, Marco snapped, 'Shut up already! You're the reason I'm in this shit in the first place. It's time we severed ties.'

Rip snickered. 'Go for it, *you* weak little tool. Give it a bash and see how far you get without me. I have full control, remember?'

Marco slumped into his chair. As quickly as he'd withered, he rose again. His face broke into a beaming smile.

'What the hell?' Kirsten asked Riaan. They were still observing him from the other room.

'This demon requires more than a shrink, my dear,' Riaan declared. Turning around, he saw Craig standing in the doorway.

'I want this to be over,' Craig said. 'I don't need all the gruesome details of our girls' murders – that can come later. I'm just asking that deranged fucker one more question, then this interrogation is done.'

Riaan stepped forward, putting a hand on Craig's shoulder. Both men turned and went into the interrogation room.

Sean and Marco were engaged in deep conversation. As Craig pulled out his chair, they stopped talking.

'I have one final question for you, Carrera,' Craig said. 'Did you murder Leigh O'Rielly, Gabriella Cantrello and Anastasia Carlyle-Benson?'

Marco looked at Sean, then half-tilted his head to the right. 'Nope. You have the wrong killer, I'm afraid.'

'Then what, may I ask, was Anastasia doing in the basement of your home? And what about all the evidence on the walls and in your cabin?'

'Oh, yes. Pardon the lapse in memory. Anastasia being at my home does ring a bell. Let me think... We did have a slight setback in my wine cellar. Rather inquisitive, that one. Too much for her own good.'

'Just answer my goddamn question!' Craig hissed. 'Did you kill them?'

'Well, I may claim responsibility for Anastasia... but then again, I may not. Whatever blows your hair back, Craig.'

Craig marched over to him and yanked him up off his chair. 'Now, fuckface, you stand up, look me in the eyes and answer my question. For the third and final time: Marco Carrera, did you kill Leigh, Gabriella, and Anastasia?'

Marco met Craig's steely stare and, with a deadpan voice, answered. 'I did. I killed them, but still have no regrets. They were my three best to date! I have such fond memories of each one's final hours.'

Without another word, Craig dropped Marco. As soon as he slammed the cell door shut, he could feel the tension in his body lift. He ordered Skye to cuff Marco and escort him to the holding cells to await sentencing.

When Craig re-entered the main area of the precinct, he was immediately swept up in Kirsten's arms. She was shaking almost as much as he was. One by one, his colleagues — Riaan, Coco, Skye, Connor, Cody, and everyone else in the precinct — surrounded them.

'You did it,' Kirsten whispered, burying her head under his chin. There were tears in both their eyes.

Chapter 36

After a heavy night of drinking, Craig was woken by the sound of his cell phone ringing at 5.30 in the morning.

Let it ring. He turned over, burying his face into his pillow. He heard the beep and knew a message had been left. *It can wait. There's nothing more important than me catching up on a little sleep this morning. I haven't felt so at peace in months.*

He pulled the duvet over his head and curled up. About ten minutes later, his phone rang again.

'For fuck's sake!' he yelled, as he got out of bed to check his phone. 'What's so important that I can't have some decent shuteye in peace? You'd think there's been a terror attack in Champaign.'

Sean Wild. Two missed calls. *Shit.*

Craig rubbed his eyes as he dialled Sean's number.

'Hello, Lieutenant,' Sean said. 'I know it's the crack of dawn, but, well... it couldn't wait. I thought you should know. I am a gentleman, after all.'

'Know what?' The familiar knot in Craig's stomach was back.

'Marco Carrera has retracted his confession.'

'On what grounds?'

'Coercion.'

'Bullshit!' he screamed. 'Counsellor, you were there. He voluntarily blurted out every gruesome detail to us, unaided and with full co-operation. What he said cannot be erased from the record.'

'Craig—'

'He *confessed!* You, me, and a whole other room of people witnessed it, and we have it all on tape! He's a murderer – that's just a fact he must live with. This will go to trial and, believe me, if he tries to tell the jury some other bullshit story, we'll simply add perjury to the equation. His admission can and will be used against him in a court of law. You know that as well as I do, Sean, so bring it on.'

'My client is sick, Lieutenant. He needs help for his condition, not to be thrown into a cage.'

'*What* condition?'

'He has dissociative identity disorder. Remember those two he mentioned, Rip and Surly?'

'Yeah?'

'They're the ones who spoke to us, not Marco. They took control of him and went on a tirade. He doesn't remember a thing.'

Craig hissed, 'You know as well as I do that Marco was the one in that room. He was fully aware of what he was doing.'

'Contrary to what science has established, Marco believes there is a proliferation of separate personalities inside him, not that his identity has fragmented. That's his story and he's sticking to it. It would be remiss in my role as his attorney not to present all·the facts of the case.'

'I won't let him get away with this,' Craig said, his voice cracking. 'You know I'll do everything in my power to make sure that the bastard pays. You don't want to be in my way.'

Sean sighed. 'I'll let you know when we have a date for the hearing.'

'Sean, you can't let him do this. I know you're his lawyer, but you *must* do something!'

'I've never lost, Lieutenant. And I don't plan on starting now. I will represent my client to the best of my ability. It's my job to get justice for Mr Carrera, and I will do just that.'

The phone clicked. Sean had hung up.

Craig felt the world spin around him. He chucked the phone at the nearest surface, hoping to hear a smash. No luck. His legs collapsed under his weight. He lay on the carpet, facedown, for what felt like hours, before he finally worked up the energy to stand up.

Luckily, he didn't have to wait long. Before noon, Sean returned his call and nonchalantly informed him that the preliminary hearing had been accelerated to top priority and would take place the next day.

+ + +

Right on schedule and armed with substantial evidence, Craig arrived at the courthouse. The seats were brimming with people. Among all the faces in the crowd, he recognised the families of Anastasia, Gabriella, and Leigh. While he walked towards the front of the courtroom, as the first witness called to the stand, he tried to give them a reassuring smile.

The deputy district attorneys convincingly established, with all the evidence they had gathered — which included hearsay testimonies from Coco, Connor, and Skye – that Marco Carrera had both motive and opportunity to commit the murders of the three girls. As a result, a finding of probable cause was made, and the court date was set for Marco's trial.

As Craig left the courtroom, satisfied with the outcome, he was met by a familiar face.

'Dad!' The stunning young woman with long auburn hair was nearly the same height as Craig, which meant that she almost barrelled him over when she rushed into his arms.

'Chelsea! What are you doing here?'

'I wanted to be here for the trial,' she said. 'For you, and for Leigh. I took a bit of time off work and booked a flight this morning. I wanted to surprise you.'

'Well, mission accomplished.' He squeezed his daughter tight. He'd been relieved that she was out of town, safe from the killer's clutches, but now he was thankful she was here. Holding her once again reminded him exactly what he was fighting for, and he mentally renewed his vow to lock up Marco Carrera for good.

Chapter 37

Marco Carrera's trial began almost a month later, on Tuesday September 7th, 2010. The prosecution looked confident – the case was solid, built primarily on witness testimonies and DNA evidence – but they were all too aware that it was never wise to underestimate the defence.

As the bailiff entered, the usual hustle and bustle happening in a courtroom prior to the commencement of a trial suddenly quietened down.

'All rise.' The crowd obeyed, the shuffling of bodies echoing in the chamber. All of Champaign – or, at least, as many as could fit in four thousand, three hundred and five square feet of it – had shown up. 'Courtroom 110 is now in session. The Hon. Thomas J. Clarkson is presiding.'

At the mention of his name, Judge Clarkson gave the room a nod, responding with a firm voice. 'Good morning.'

Everyone settled into their respective positions. The counsel tables were abuzz with the shuffling of files, and the occasional cough sounded in the background. Taking charge of the prosecution team was the highly respected Frederick Sansom, with his fellow deputy district attorney Elias A. Cassirley at his side.

Standing tall and poised, Frederick began his opening statement. With masterful eloquence, he painted a vivid picture of the case. He exuded an air of authority and amiability, conveying his theories with unwavering conviction.

Sean Wild adopted a divergent tactic for the defence. He began his statement by launching a full-frontal assault, mentioning that the prosecution had speculated that the first two crime scenes bore Marco's fingerprints, despite their being only partial prints, and had insinuated that his prints were discovered at the third crime scene. Sean emphasised the fact that there was a legitimate explanation for that, as Marco resided in that house.

Both the prosecution and defence had several witnesses. Over the ensuing weeks, some delivered compelling testimonies, while others weren't so persuasive. A few blows were dealt when reputable members of the community testified on Marco's behalf. On the stand, they were unwavering in their conviction that the police had arrested the wrong person.

This high-profile case garnered extensive media attention. Every network was on-site and highly visible. This trial was headline news in all the newspapers across the country and was unequivocally the leading story on each TV news bulletin.

At one point, Sebastian was called to the stand.

'Mr Hampton,' Sean said, pacing back and forth in front of the podium. 'Tell me about your relationship with Ms Gabriella Cantrello.'

He shrugged. 'We were friends back in high school when we were in the same drama class.'

'The drama class attended by the three victims and taught by Mr Carrera?'

'Yes,' Sebastian said, grimacing.

'And what about in the ten years since you left school? Did you have any contact with Ms Cantrello or the other victims?'

'No. Not really.'

'Not really? Please clarify, Mr Hampton.'

'I mean... well, I saw Gabriella around, but we never talked or anything like that.'

'And what do you say to the rumours that you were obsessed with Ms Cantrello? That you were stalking her.'

There was mumbling from the crowd, and from the jury. Sebastian's face got redder by the second; it wouldn't be long before he snapped.

'Well, I'd say the rumours were bullshit, Mr Wild,' Sebastian said through gritted teeth.

'You were mad that she rejected your advances, weren't you? You thought that if you couldn't have her, no one could.'

Frederick shot to his feet. 'Objection!'

'Sustained,' Judge Clarkson said.

Sebastian hit his palm on the stand. 'I *loved* Gabriella!'

'Is that why you killed her?' Sean asked, eyes narrow.

Sebastian was coming undone. 'I–'

'Mr Wild, please refrain from badgering the witness.'

'Yes, Your Honour.' Sean readjusted his sky-blue tie. 'Alright. Mr Hampton, did you or did you not own the purple rug in question?'

'I did, but may I remind the court that this rug was given to me by Marco Carrera,' Sebastian said.

'However, Mr Hampton, may I remind *you* that you are under oath and the rug was in your possession at the time of Ms Leigh O'Rielly's murder.' Sean pointed his finger at Sebastian.

Sebastian hesitated. That was enough for Sean.

'Mr Hampton, is it possible that this rug and your dog were part of a plan you had crafted to eliminate the beautiful, innocent Leigh O'Rielly?'

'Objection!'

'Sustained,' Judge Clarkson said, this time directing a pointed look at Sean. 'Keep it civil, Mr Wild.'

'There is cold, hard evidence that your DNA is all over it,' Sean continued in a rather cocky tone.

'You can bring the Bible back here right now, and I'll swear on it that I did not commit this heinous crime!'

Sebastian said. 'And… well… to the best of my knowledge, I hadn't seen that rug in a while.'

Sean raised one eyebrow. 'I am only concerned about the facts, Mr Hampton. The facts are straightforward: your rug was found at a murder scene. There are nine dead women. It's highly probable that an innocent man has been unjustly accused.'

'Get to the point, Mr Wild,' Judge Clarkson said.

Sean looked over his shoulder at the jury. 'No further questions, Your Honour.'

'Your Honour,' Frederick said. 'I respectfully request side bar!'

Judge Clarkson instructed counsel to approach the bench. There were hushed whispers – what sounded like muted shouting – before the counsellors returned to their positions.

'At this time,' Judge Clarkson said, 'we'll take a fifteen-minute recess. Mr Hampton, step down.'

Sebastian looked grateful as he left the stand and pushed through the crowd, weaving his way towards the door. A few more witnesses testified after the recess, then court adjourned for the day.

'Well,' Kirsten said to Craig and Chelsea, as they walked down the court steps, 'if today was any indication, at least we know it won't be a boring trial.'

Chapter 38

The following morning continued with more witnesses. First off, Marco Carrera's neighbour, Judy Murphy, was called to the stand.

'So,' Sean began, 'on the day of Anastasia Carlyle-Benson's murder, you were next door and heard a commotion at Mr Carrera's house.'

'Yes,' Judy affirmed, her strong Irish accent colouring her words. 'I heard two people, and it sounded like they were arguing. There was screaming coming from that house. One voice was female, and the other was male.'

'Was the male a mature individual with an accent?'

'This is cause for speculation, Your Honour,' Frederick interjected.

'Sustained. Foundational.'

'Alright,' Sean said. 'The male voice you heard: did he have a foreign accent? More specifically, was it a Latino accent?'

'I can't say. Every accent is foreign to me.'

'Highly unlikely that an accent can be picked up at that range, Your Honour,' Frederick said.

The trial had become tedious. Countless irrelevant inquiries were being made, and redundant facts were being reiterated. The lawyers representing each side were becoming agitated, frequently interrupting one another. Judge Clarkson had grown irritated with both parties and, before they could begin to argue again, he abruptly cut them off, his voice booming through the courtroom.

'Enough! I will not allow this inappropriate behaviour in my courtroom. I'm about to hold the two of you in contempt.' He shook his head. 'Let's take a recess and see if you can cool off. We will resume in ten minutes. Ms Murphy, you may step down.'

As his voice echoed through the room, the onlookers fell silent. The attorneys stared in shock at the normally composed judge, unsure of how to react. His sudden outburst was unexpected, but it had successfully refocused everyone's attention back to the matter at hand.

The tension in the atmosphere lingered. Craig and Kirsten sat on the edges of their seats, fully engrossed in the ongoing cross-examinations. As the next witness took the stand, they both leaned forward in anticipation — it was the coroner Barry Blake's turn.

Frederick launched the initial inquiry. 'Can you provide me with your overview and analysis of all the deceased individuals involved?'

Adjusting his moustache, Barry straightened his back. 'Four of the out-of-state victims' bones display incisions that match those made by a dismemberment tool.'

'What else did you observe about all the out-of-state victims, as well as our three Champaign girls, Leigh, Gabriella, and Anastasia?'

'The distinguishing feature is the rough, uneven severing of their left earlobes,' Barry explained. 'Additionally, I would like to mention that the murderer has surgical expertise that surpasses anything I have seen previously.'

The prosecution concluded their interrogation with one final question.

'In brief, what were your findings from the post-mortem examination?'

'The cause of death in all three cases was strangulation using a ligature looped around the victims' necks, pulled by a dynamic power. All three victims had cerebral hypoxia due to the compression of blood vessels in their brains. Internal examination of two victims revealed bruises on the left side of the tongue and at its base, as well as in the left neck muscles. All three sustained multiple stab wounds. I believe that all three instances of homicidal violence were carried out by the same individual.'

Gasps and sighs resonated throughout the court.

'No further questions, Your Honour,' Frederick stated, as he turned to return to his seat.

Sean stood up. 'Doctor, in your own words, could you explain how distinct the alleged surgical abilities were compared to what you usually observe?'

Barry was clearly caught off guard by this question and responded hesitantly. 'Well, it's hard to answer that in one go. It is my opinion that the dissections weren't consistent with what is taught in medical school; nevertheless, there appears to be some knowledge of surgical techniques.'

Sean's forehead creased. 'So, would it be fair to assume that the suspect may be a doctor?'

'That is a possibility,' he conceded. 'However, it isn't what I was suggesting.'

'No further questions, Your Honour.'

Chapter 39

In the sombre halls of the courtroom, the families of the nine slain girls watched the proceedings with heaviness in their hearts, glued to their seats every single day of the trial. Their stories and losses were unique, but they shared the common thread of tragedy and injustice.

Francesca Cantrello had grown much stronger since her cardiac ordeal, though she still wept every time she heard her precious daughter's name. She maintained her poise, beautifully made up to exemplify her operatic looks, right down to her waterproof black eyeliner and bright red lips. Pepe stayed by her side, rubbing circles on her back, and holding her hand tightly, constantly having to muster his own strength for her to draw from.

All of Gabriella's brothers were there, supporting their parents. Adriano was the strongest emotionally among the siblings. Leonardo listened attentively to all the cross-examinations, barely breathing in case he missed a word. Franco had flown in his wife, Valentina, from San Remo. She had been exceptionally close to Gabriella; they'd been more like sisters than in-laws.

Alessandro was the most visibly distraught of them all. Losing Gabriella had been like losing a twin. Throughout the trial, he and Bjorn sat together, shoulder to shoulder, providing silent comfort and support. Alessandro would occasionally offer Bjorn a murmur of sympathy. He was probably one of the only people who understood what the other man was going through – but Bjorn had barely spoken a single word to anyone.

Lily Carlyle took advantage of her fifteen minutes of fame by flaunting a new ensemble from her designer wardrobe every day as she arrived at the courthouse. Her fashion choices ranged from the high-end to the bold and teasingly trash-tastic, often garnering disapproving glances from more conservative onlookers. She occasionally draped a modest pashmina over her shoulders, and she constantly adjusted the revealing straps of her top and tousled her flowing locks. Nobody was more aware of the cameras than she was. Brady, cognisant of the vulnerability under his wife's facade, protected her. Patrick, her other pillar of strength, was also at her side, mirroring his father.

In stark contrast, Shelagh O'Rielly maintained her signature grace and poise throughout the trial. She was always impeccably dressed in tailored suits and sensible heels, and her hairdo never had a strand out of place. Her friendship with Kirsten was evident in their shared elegance. Despite her deep sorrow, she exuded an aura of dignity. Dylan held his wife tightly and comforted her as she grieved, holding back his own tears.

Astrid Larsson clutched photos of her long-lost precious Ava, her face pale and gaunt. Her doting husband Lars epitomised strength as he wrapped her in his arms, stroking her forehead every so often. Celeste Hunter shook with anger, tears streaming down her tanned cheeks, as she faced her beloved daughter Mia's killer, never looking away from the nefarious Marco. Mia's identical twin Nessie was embroiled in a silent, deep pain, having experienced the ultimate loss of her soulmate. Life to her would never, ever be the same. Regret consumed her as she couldn't forgive herself for skipping the mall trip with Mia that day.

Rossi Galburche's countless sleepless nights in mourning left her eyes hollow and red, revealing the weight of her grief. In a total daze, her gaze drifting without focus. Seated in silence, Hazel Baker's shoulders slumped under the burden of her emotions. The surroundings echoed with muffled sobs and the gentle rustle of tissues from her handbag. Beneath his coat, her husband Howard, enveloped her in a warm and comforting embrace. Deborah and David Welsh sat huddled together, their faces etched with the raw pain of loss. Their tears spilled over unashamedly as they struggled to hold onto any semblance of hope. Therese Evans's cries for justice rang out, aching and heart-wrenching, her brokenness stretching beyond herself, seeping into her fiancé, Arthur.

Yet, amidst all the sadness, there was also an unmistakable sense of unity among them. They sat together, shoulder to shoulder, as a show of solidarity. Even though each family had lost a different person, they shared a common bond of grief and loss that no one else in the room could truly understand. The courtroom seemed to shrink in on itself as if suffocating in the presence of such unspeakable tragedy.

It was a sombre scene, but it was also a powerful one. A room full of families who had suffered the ultimate loss, but who were determined to persevere, united in their search for justice, healing, and closure.

The next day would be rougher than most; the trial had reached its final day of witness testimonies before closing arguments. The prosecution appeared to be winning, but with the unpredictable nature of the law, the outcome remained uncertain.

Judge Clarkson ordered Marco to take the stand at the prosecution's insistence.

'Good afternoon, Mr Carrera,' the judge said.

'Good afternoon, Your Honour,' Marco replied.

'Please remember that you are still under oath. Mr Sansom, you may proceed.'

'Thank you, Your Honour,' said Frederick. 'Mr Carrera, was your testimony during the preliminary hearing entirely truthful?'

Marco kept his gaze down. 'I wish to assert my Fifth Amendment privilege.' A rush of disbelief echoed through the courtroom.

'Have you ever given false testimony?'

Again, Marco refused to look up. 'I plead the Fifth Amendment,' he repeated.

Frederick sighed. 'Do you plan on invoking your Fifth Amendment right for all my questions?'

Finally, Marco raised his head and stared intently at Frederick. 'Yes.'

'No further questions,' Frederick said.

Sean stood up. 'Given that Mr Carrera has indicated he will not answer any questions, we will not subject him to further examination today. It has been established that he is in a delicate state and not capable of withstanding cross-examination. I only hope the court will show mercy towards my client and take this into consideration.'

'Very well,' Judge Clarkson said. 'Mr Carrera, you may step down from the stand and join your team.'

The prosecution had kept their ace up their sleeve for the grand finale. Despite the rollercoaster of emotions throughout the past few weeks of testimonies, they were convinced that their next witness could secure their victory. Frederick had asked for Ms Ethel Fensham, an expert forensic biologist, to take the stand.

'Ms Fensham,' Frederick said, 'can you explain to the court the inherent qualities of DNA?'

'The information within DNA is stored as a code comprised of four chemical bases: adenine, thymine, guanine, and cytosine,' Ethel said. 'These are shortened to their initial letters, A, T, G, and C. They combine with one another – A with T and C with G – to form base pairs. As a result, no two individuals have the same DNA, except for identical twins.'

She held the undivided attention of everyone in the courtroom. It was the first time Marco had displayed any form of trepidation, visibly biting his fingernails to the quick.

'Ms Fensham, although these specifics may appear perplexing to someone without scientific knowledge, the findings are remarkably accurate in matching a suspect to microscopic traces left at a crime scene. Would you concur?'

'Without a doubt. The matching process is more than a million times more precise than fingerprinting.'

'Over a million times more precise than fingerprinting? Amazing. And what were the results of the blood analysis at the theatre crime scene, Ms Fensham?'

'The analysis of the RFLP pattern from Item Sixteen indicates–'

'Allow me to rephrase. Did this exceptionally precise DNA matching uncover anyone else's DNA at the site of the murders, aside from that of the three victims?'

'Yes, there was one other person.'

'And does this DNA correspond with the blood discovered on the purple rug at the ravine?'

'Indeed, it does.'

'And does it correspond with the blood you discovered in Marco Carrera's car trunk?'

'Yes.'

'And does it correspond with the DNA and blood you discovered in Marco Carrera's basement?'

'Yes,' Ethel stated, appearing quite exhausted by the prolonged questioning. 'It is all from the same individual's DNA profile.'

Frederick recognised the impact this was having on her but needed a few more answers. 'Is it possible for this DNA to belong to anyone else, Ms Fensham?'

'Highly unlikely. That blood sample has a specific set of characteristics that could only exist in roughly one in a hundred and forty million individuals.' She wiped her forehead.

'One person out of a hundred and forty million!' Frederick said, a slight smile on his face. 'Goodness, that is quite astounding. Is the individual whose DNA matches all of that in this courtroom today, Ms Fensham?'

'Yes.'

'Very well. Could you please identify this person to the jury?'

She raised her arm, pointing at Marco.

'Let the record show that Ms Ethel Fensham is identifying the defendant, Mr Marco Carrera. Your Honour, I have no further questions.'

Sean cross-examined the witness, but he could not refute the forensic findings. The evidence was much too incriminating. When he was finished, the courtroom erupted in a torrent of murmurs beyond anyone's control.

The prosecution presented their final witness: the young girl who'd been discovered bound in chains inside the cabin, Piper Shaw. Piper displayed obvious signs of trauma and appeared visibly shaken by the prospect of facing her captor again. Despite this, she showed incredible bravery, as she answered each question, although she remained nervous and didn't make eye contact.

Frederick made a compelling argument that Piper would've been the tenth victim if not for the efforts of Craig and the SWAT teams who'd rescued her from the dungeon-like basement. Piper's DNA had been found throughout the cabin, particularly on the chains, knife, and operating table in the basement. Marco's attempt to escape was the final nail in the coffin.

Sean claimed that Piper had willingly climbed into Marco's car and remained with him in the cabin without attempting to escape. He tried to assert that her presence there had been consensual, but the jury did not believe him.

'Mr Sansom,' said Judge Clarkson, 'will there be any further witnesses called?'

'No, Your Honour,' Frederick said. 'The prosecution rests.'

The defence started packing up early. 'Mr Wild?' inquired the judge.

'The defence also rests, Your Honour,' replied Sean, with an air of dejection.

Chapter 40

The following morning, it was finally time for closing arguments. As the burden of proof was on the prosecution, Frederick stood up first. This was his chance to respond to Sean's arguments and make a final plea to the jury. He sensed that many of them were already leaning in his favour, but this last opportunity could seal their victory.

While Frederick approached the front of the court, Craig felt Kirsten's nails – perfectly polished and sharp – dig into his skin. He took her hand and held it tightly.

'Ladies and gentlemen,' Frederick began. 'This has been a difficult trial for all of us. Nine precious lives have been taken. The final three victims were high-profile, and the accused was someone we all trusted. Don't they all deserve justice? We have proven that Marco Carrera was present at Leigh, Gabriella, and Anastasia's crime scenes, even if he wasn't the killer. DNA evidence doesn't lie.'

Frederick paced in front of the stand, weighing his words carefully. 'Carrera had the motive and the means to commit these heinous crimes. He intimately involved himself in the lives of all three of the Golden Trio. I urge you to think of Leigh, Gabriella, and Anastasia today. Many of you in this courtroom knew them personally, and you know that they deserved the best. Since we cannot give that to them, the least we can do is ensure that the monster who preyed on them as teenagers, who earned their trust only to betray them, faces the consequences of his actions.'

He turned to the jury. 'Justice must be served. Please do what's right for Champaign's golden girls. Thank you.'

Francesca's sobs reverberated through the silent chamber. Though the other two mothers' cries couldn't be heard, tears streamed down their faces.

Sean rose from the bench and made his way to the front, waiting a few moments for the women's weeping to subside before he commenced his oration.

'While the prosecution appears to be resolute about Mr Carrera's culpability, I do not believe that they have conclusively proven that the man in front of you was the perpetrator. You all know Marco Carrera. Many of his allies and advocates are present today!'

He gestured to the audience, then pivoted, and stared at Frederick.

'I concur with Mr Sansom in that the responsible party needs to be brought to justice. The tragedies that have befallen our city in the past few months have been nothing less than abhorrent. But let me remind the court that just because we are bloodthirsty does not mean we should jump to conclusions! Other DNA evidence was discovered at the crime scene: Mr Hampton's. He can be linked to two of the three victims and has a record of brutality – that surely raises doubt. Now, I do not want to accuse Mr Hampton.'

Craig snickered, as did a few other onlookers.

'Fine,' Sean said, 'not *entirely*. However, if the authorities are willing to disregard relevant evidence to implicate the defendant, then I would suggest that the entire case should be re-examined with fresh eyes, wouldn't you say?'

Craig ground his teeth at the very idea. As much as he loathed to acknowledge it, Sean was a compelling speaker. And, at present, he was being utterly blunt.

'Moreover, we haven't even considered his condition! I don't believe we should punish a man for his mental illness. How can we put him on trial when he is forced to do things beyond his control? If Mr Carrera is indeed guilty of any of the murders he is accused of, then there is one simple truth: he needs a doctor, not a cell. This entire exhibition, this mistreatment of a man who is already suffering, is frankly nauseating. You want a scapegoat; believe me, I understand. But Marco Carrera being an easy target who may have gotten swept up in this mess does not justify you pulling the trigger.'

Sean drew a deep breath before staring directly at each juror in turn. He was never the first to look away.

'All I request is that you ponder your actions. Three lives have been lost in the past few months, and numerous others have been decimated over the previous decades. Why must we add one more to that list when we can never truly know if he was at fault?'

With a sweeping gesture, Sean returned to his seat. The jury retired to commence their deliberations. Some members were eager to vote immediately, split between advocating for Marco's guilt or innocence. However, others were unsure, recognising the weight of the verdict and the gravity of sentencing an individual to nine life sentences. Although the jurors were unfamiliar with Marco and the victims, they understood that any misstep could result in national scrutiny and repercussions, so they were meticulous in their approach.

After appointing their foreperson, they agreed to allow each juror to present their reasoning before examining the evidence in-depth. It took them an additional three days to thoroughly evaluate all the details.

'What do you think they're doing in there?' Craig asked Kirsten. They were in his office, defiantly smoking and sitting by the phone. 'It doesn't take a fucking genius to know he killed those girls.'

'Hush,' she said, smacking him lightly. 'Just be patient.'

By the fourth day, the panel had reached a verdict. The Hon. Thomas J. Clarkson reconvened proceedings. The courtroom was packed with spectators eager to hear the decision.

'Has the jury agreed on a verdict?' the bailiff asked the speaker.

'Yes, we have.'

The silence was deafening while everyone waited in anticipation.

'We, the jury, find the defendant, Marco Carrera, guilty on all nine counts of first-degree murder.'

The audience erupted in applause. Twenty years after the first victim was slain, the monster who took nine innocent young women's lives and eluded authorities for decades would finally be brought to justice.

'Order! Order!' Judge Clarkson yelled, waiting for the room to settle. It took a while, but eventually, the crowd was reduced to murmurs. 'Marco Carrera, as much as I would love for you to spend nine consecutive life sentences in prison, I feel that even that is too good for you. You are certainly not fit to venture back into society; quite frankly, you are the most vile, despicable creature I have ever had the displeasure of sentencing in all my years in this profession.'

Jeers echoed throughout the chamber.

'I sentence you to death by lethal injection.'

Craig felt vindicated, even though he knew it wouldn't bring back the girls. He was comforted by the knowledge that Marco couldn't exact such evil again. That made it all worthwhile. He believed in the integrity of the justice system, knowing that its primary responsibility was to protect innocent individuals and discover the truth.

They sure nailed it, he thought, as he glanced towards the prosecution. He and Frederick shared a smile, acknowledging their mutual respect.

'Now,' Judge Clarkson said, 'please get this man out of my courtroom.'

One could sense the burden being lifted from all the families while Marco was escorted out of the courtroom in restraints. Francesca wept once more, but this time, her tears seemed to be tears of relief.

As Marco approached the exit, he turned around and cracked a wry smile. Craig reciprocated.

'I'll make sure to pay you a visit in the hole, Carrera, before your big day. And then I'll be in the front row at your execution, standing up and approaching the window as they inject you, ensuring that my face is etched into your memory forever. You'll burn in hell, you savage, and I'll be the last person you'll ever lay eyes on. Who'll be laughing then?'

Marco tilted his head. 'Your daughter… she's quite beautiful, isn't she?'

Craig froze. 'What the fuck did you just say?'

'I can imagine her screams would be just as delightful. Can you picture it, Craig? I sure can. It'll get me through many cold and lonely days in the big house while I wait for you.'

Craig tried to attack him, but a mountain of a security guard blocked him. 'You can't touch the defendant, sir.'

'That piece of shit threatened my daughter!' He hurled himself yet again at the guard, who appeared unperturbed.

'I'll be waiting for your visit, Lieutenant!' Marco yelled. 'Oh and bring Chelsea with you.'

All Craig heard as Marco was taken away was the sound of his laughter growing until it resounded through the courtroom.

Alessandro had witnessed the confrontation between Craig and Marco. He stood in the shadows, clutching the worn Swiss Army knife concealed in his jacket, a gift from Gabriella many years before.

'I'll make you pay for what you did to my sister, you bastard,' he hissed menacingly and moved forward with measured, deliberate steps, closing the distance with intent.

Glossary

Pg 88	*Caro mia*	My dear
Pg 89	*Fattore dominante*	Dominant factor
	Ciao,buon pomeriggio	Hello, good afternoon
Pg 90	*Buon appetite*	Enjoy your meal
Pg 159	*Mia bella bambina*	My beautiful little girl
Pg 173	*Si*	Yes
Pg 173	*Aeroporto*	Airport
Pg 183	*Signor*	Mr
	Si vergognino	Shame on them
	Vieni con me mia bella	Come with me my beautiful
Pg 183	*Mia bella, Italia il mio bel paese, e Il migliore al mondo*	My beautiful, Italy my beautiful country, and the best in the world
Pg 214	*Non capisco*	I do not understand
	Assolutamente	Absolutely
	Ora e il momento di prepararsi per la serata	Now it's time to get ready for the evening
Pg 215	*Bevanda preferita*	Favourite drink
Pg 221	*Perche*	Why
	Perche mia bella	Why my beautiful
Pg 225	*Stronzo*	Asshole

Pg 240	*Il mio bel bambina preso da me in un modo scandaloso*	My beautiful baby taken from me in a scandalous way
	Non posso accettare questo, non posso prendere il dolore	I cannot accept this, I cannot take the pain
Pg 259	*congratulazioni*	Congratulations
	Grazie mille	Thank you so much

Acknowledgements

It took eight years of intermittent work and eighteen drafts for this book to reach you. Talk about not rushing it!

Once this book had developed from a concept in my head to a manuscript ready to publish, there were a few people involved who deserve to be thanked.

To my amazing crew who helped me get this book into your hands: Sarah Ayres, Jennifer Althaus, Evan Shapiro, and Cristy Zinn.

To my precious children and grandchildren, thank you for being you and making me so proud. Your unwavering belief in me means everything.

To my wonderful, loving husband and best friend, thank you for giving me the freedom to write.

To my late darling dad, thank you for your love and care through the years. I love and miss you. I couldn't have done it without your (and Mom's) genetic material!

To my special brother, thank you for your loyal support and wandering the meandering path of life with me.

Finally, I'd like to thank you, my cherished readers. The thought of you holding this book in your hands gives me immense joy. It is an incredible, unexpected gift which will forever keep me grounded.

P.S. To anyone who thinks I might have written about them, maybe I did!

www.ingramcontent.com/pod-product-compliance
Lightning Source LLC
Chambersburg PA
CBHW020542120726
47903CB00001B/91